SHADOW OF THE HUNTER

Melody waited for her father to come out of prison knowing that he would be a changed man. But she didn't expect that she herself would become a target for the predators of the underworld. Her father had been found guilty of stealing a fortune in jewels—jewels which had never been found. And more than one person wanted to get their hands on them . . .

SHADOW OF THE HUNTER

Melody waited for her father to come out of prison knowing that he would be a changed man. But she didn't expect that she herself would become a target for the predators of the underworld. Her father had been found guilty of stealing a fortune in jewels—jewels which had never been found. And more than one person wanted to get their hands on them . . .

CAROLE KERR

SHADOW OF THE HUNTER

Complete and Unabridged

LINFORD
Leicester

First published in Great Britain in 1975 by
Robert Hale Ltd.,
London

First Linford Mystery Edition
published July 1987

British Library CIP Data

Kerr, Carole
    Shadow of the hunter.—Large print ed.—
Linford mystery library
    Rn: Margaret Carr   I. Title
    823'.914[F]   PR6053.A694/

    ISBN 0-7089-6393-5

Published by
F. A. Thorpe (Publishing) Ltd.
Anstey, Leicestershire
Set by Rowland Phototypesetting Ltd.
Bury St. Edmunds, Suffolk
Printed and bound in Great Britain by
T. J. Press (Padstow) Ltd., Padstow, Cornwall

MELODY waited in the car park where she could see the gates of the prison. She was early. She knew it but didn't care. What were minutes compared with years? He hadn't let her visit him—not after that first time. His daughter was not to be degraded and humiliated. She was his beloved, to be protected and sheltered.

She stood leaning against the car, a slender figure even in the bulky fur coat she was wearing. A jaunty fur cap was perched on her head and stray golden tendrils of hair escaped to curl along her cheeks. She had a delicate, somewhat wistful face and her eyes were anxious as she waited.

It was a cold day, with frost glistening on the ground and catching in the sunlight on the high walls that seemed to meet the sky. Her breath streamed out into the air. But it wasn't the temperature that made her shiver.

The waiting was nearly over. In a short time those huge prison gates would swing open and her father would be free to walk out. She had steeled herself to expect change. What man wouldn't change? Caged in a prison cell, hemmed in by bars and locks and those high walls. He had hated confinement of any kind; rules, regulations, petty restrictions—he had laughed at them. But it wouldn't have been so easy to laugh these last two and a half years. She had seen the confidence drain away during those days of the trial, the stunned disbelief that people could think he was a thief. He had taken the necklace home admittedly. He had wanted Melody to see it, to feel it around her throat. A ten thousand pound collar of diamonds, part of the famous Galbreith collection. How many girls had a chance to feel like a princess, if only for a very short time? He had meant to take it back the next morning. Only the police had arrived before then. They had hammered on the door in the middle of the night and they had taken him away when they found the necklace.

She blinked. A man had materialised—it seemed out of thin air. And then as he took a step forward, she saw the miniature doorway inset in those big gates. It slammed shut with a sound that cracked like a whip on the frosty air.

The man stood still, as if unable to believe he was free to move. He took his first hesitant steps with a glance over his shoulder.

Melody found she could not move. Was this her father? This oddly shrunken man who walked as if he were afraid? His camel coat was far too big for him and his hair was silver where her father's had been a deep black.

She closed her eyes visualising the big vital man who had been her father; she saw him as he had been that last night, his eyes alight with laughter and pride as he put the necklace around her neck. The stones had been cold on her skin and then he had turned her around to face the mirror and she had been stunned into silence.

Fire and ice, sparkling brilliance, facets of pure light that dazzled and bemused.

"That's how they should be worn," her father said. "With youth and beauty." His hands were on her shoulders and he sounded sad. "You're going to break a lot of hearts, my lovely. In another couple of years you'll be forgetting all about me."

She had merely smiled. Forget him? No one could ever make that happen. In the years following her mother's death they had grown very close.

She knew he was no thief. She knew it with every fibre of her being.

She went forward, diffidently at first and then at a run. It *was* her father. She saw his face light up and then she was in his arms.

She could feel the hammering of his heart as she pressed her head against his chest, seeking the reassurance his arms had always given her. The tears were streaming down her face. He had stopped dead when she ran towards him, his face working for a moment before he managed to smile. For a horrible moment she had thought he was going to break down. His skin was a grey pallid colour and there were deep lines around his mouth and eyes.

"My lovely," he said, and there was a queer rasp in his voice. "It's all right." He held her away from him. "Let me look at you. You've grown up."

"I should think so. I'm nearly twenty now." She tried to smile and he smoothed away her tears with his shapely jeweller's fingers that could work with such delicacy and skill.

"They didn't have you sewing mailbags then?"

He jerked his hands away abruptly. "No. They don't do that any more. I don't want to talk about it, Melody. Not ever. Let's get away from here."

She blinked hard and said brightly, "I've borrowed the car from Aunt Prudence."

"You can drive?"

There was astonishment and what

seemed like dismay in his voice. She swallowed the flippant answer. He wasn't ready for that, not yet. There were adjustments to be made. The world had stopped for him when he started his prison sentence. It must be hard for him to realise that it hadn't stopped for everyone else.

"I passed my test last year," she said.

"Who taught you?"

So that was it as well. Another man had taken over his role.

"I went to a school. Aunt Prudence said it would be a useful accomplishment."

"She was always the sensible one," her father said. "Not like me." And he sighed. "You've been all right with her, haven't you?"

"Yes, of course. She's been marvellous to us."

"And how is Michael?"

Michael was her younger brother. He'd just started at grammar school when his father was arrested and he had suffered deeply. He hadn't wanted to see his

6

father, he had disowned him completely. The last week had been a horrible one. Michael, tight-lipped and morose, his brooding silence broken by violent outbursts. Why did he have to come here? . . . Spoiling their life again. He was a thief . . . They didn't want him . . . They didn't need him . . . They could get along fine without him.

Aunt Prudence, briskly assertive, standing for no nonsense. He had to come here . . . for a little while at least. Until he finds his feet again.

She was Peter Ford's sister, the reverse side of the coin. Practical, business-like, efficient. She taught English at one of the local high schools and the only way in which she and her brother were alike was in their basic kindness.

Melody couldn't imagine her aunt hurting anyone's feelings. She might believe her brother had taken the jewels, heaven knew there was reason enough. They had shown that at the trial. Their beautiful home mortgaged to the hilt, the debts, the extravagances. Easy enough to understand why he had succumbed to the sudden temptation.

Yet Aunt Prudence had remained loyal. She had been there when they needed her. And she alone had been the one to visit her father in prison. If it had been hard for her she had never let them know it.

Michael had come to love her as the mother he had barely known. He has always been conscious that Melody was his father's favourite and it had made him resentful and a little rebellious even before his father's arrest.

"He's at a difficult age," Melody said soberly. "You'll have to be patient with him."

"He doesn't want to know me," her father said. He got in the car and sat beside her. "I suppose I can hardly blame him." There was a bleak acceptance in him that wrung her heart.

"You didn't do it," she said fiercely. "You've nothing to be ashamed of."

"You still believe in me? After all this time?" He shook his head, smiling

8

tiredly. "But of course you would. You were always loyal. The only one."

"Don't talk like that. I'm not the only one. You have a lot of friends who still believe in you. You just have to give them a chance to show it. And the judge would have given you a far heavier sentence if he'd not had any doubts."

"Oh, Melody . . . Don't talk such foolishness. He—Well, it doesn't matter. Have you seen Miles at all?"

"Once." Her face tightened. Miles Mathieson, her father's partner. The one who had discovered the jewels were missing and phoned the police. He was the only man besides her father who knew the combination of the safe.

She had gone to him, accused him point blank of taking them himself. He hadn't been angry. She would have felt better if he had been. He was always controlled, never out of countenance. He had told her earnestly that there had been no thought in his mind that her father could have had anything to do with the theft. It was the police who had jumped to conclusions and acted so precipitately. And the damning thing, of course, had been the diamond necklace in her father's possession.

The Galbreith Jewels were well known. Natalie Galbreith had known her father and it was at her instigation that the jewels came to them for re-valuation when her mother-in-law died. They had been insured for £100,000. She thought they were worth more. Miles agreed with her. He and Peter Ford had spent the afternoon examining them. Old Mrs. Galbreith bought jewels not merely as an investment but for their beauty. There wasn't a jewel in the collection that wasn't of the first water.

Mrs. Mathieson loved jewels too. She had persuaded her husband to show them to her that night and after a late dinner he had taken her into town.

He told Melody it was the biggest shock of his life when he opened the safe and found them missing. There were no signs of a break in, no sign of the safe having been tampered with. "There are professionals though, who don't leave traces," he said. "Don't worry about your father. The police will sort it all out."

That was before the trial. He had taken the stand, he had sworn that he didn't believe Peter Ford was guilty.

But Peter had been the last to leave the premises that night. He'd had the opportunity, the motive, and the diamond necklace.

Miles had gone straight home that night. He'd caught his usual train, travelled with a neighbour and then been with his wife until the moment he opened the safe. There had been no opportunity for him to take the jewels and he wasn't in debt. He lived quietly and modestly with his wife and his bank account was in a healthy state. They had no daughter to squander money on, no wealthy friends to keep up with, and he'd been the one to call in the police.

"Are you going to see him?" she asked her father. "Do you think he's the one who took the rest of the collection?"

"I don't see how he could have done."

Her father was silent for a moment. "They've not turned up, not anywhere. They all think I've got them hidden somewhere."

"They?"

"The police . . . the people in prison. There's a kind of grapevine that operates in there. People talk. If anyone had tried to sell them, even abroad, word would have filtered through. Crime is a business, there are people trained in the different fields just as a student specialises in college in one particular subject. I never believed—" He broke off. "Start the car, Melody. Quickly."

"Why?" But she was already doing as he said. There was a note of alarm, even fear in his voice.

She shot out of the car park and into the line of traffic.

Her father kept his eyes on the road behind them.

She burst through a light already on red and scuttled round into a side street going flat out until another road presented itself. There was nothing behind them then.

"You went to a good school," her father said and for a brief moment the old familiar note was back in his voice; the humorous inflection lightly covering his pride, and then the tired drag took over again.

"I've failed you, Melody." The anguish was barely concealed.

"I'll have to go away—where no one can find me."

"What on earth are you talking about?"

"They think I know where the jewels are."

"Who? And who did you think was following us?"

"I'm edgy. It was probably nothing. Where are we going?"

"Home." But it wasn't home. Not to her father. That was another mistake. They had no home now. It had gone, along with everything else. "I'm going to cook you a special lunch," she said. "Weiner Schnitzel. Is it still your favourite?"

"I've forgotten what it's like." He turned around again, glancing over his shoulder worriedly. A lorry had fallen in behind them. He watched it, relaxing as it slowed and stopped outside a warehouse.

Melody turned back onto the main road again, driving sedately in the line of traffic.

Aunt Prudence lived on the other side of town, in a neat semi-detached house with a prim lawn at the front and the back, surrounded by rose trees.

She was out at school when they got back but there was a bowl of flowers on the table that hadn't been there when Melody left the house. She must have slipped back in a free period. There were flowers in her father's room too, tawny chrysanthemums.

Melody took him up with some reluctance. It was a far cry from the bedroom that had been his in their spacious home. She had wanted him to have her own room but Aunt Prudence had refused to consider it for a moment.

"He wouldn't want to turn you out," she had said, and that was the end of the matter. She had bought a narrow single bed and curtained off the recess by the window and there was just room for a little chest of drawers under the window.

Melody had filled the drawers with her father's shirts and underclothes, taken three of his favourite suits to the cleaners and hung them carefully behind the curtain. Most of his clothes were still in the packing cases stored in the cellar. He had been a fastidious dresser. Aunt Prudence had considered selling some of them but decided it wouldn't be worth it. She had sold all their furniture, anything that could be considered valuable. But that had been what her father had wanted.

"It's quite a comfortable bed," she assured her father. "I tried it."

He had crossed at once to the window and was standing behind the curtain looking out, glancing down the wide avenue with its trees and grass verges and then across at the houses opposite. It was a pleasant neighbourhood, slightly complacent about its respectability.

"Do they know?" he said.

She didn't pretend to misunderstand him. "They must do, some of them. No one's ever said anything though. Every one has a healthy respect for Aunt Prudence. She can reduce anyone to a state of shattered paralysis with a few well chosen words."

"I can imagine it." He turned away. "I've been looking forward to a bath."

"The water's hot. Aunt Prudence had central heating installed last year. It's gas and very efficient. You'll find plenty of towels in the airing cupboard."

Downstairs she poured a generous whisky and soda, placed it beside the box of cigarettes she'd bought and turned the fire on.

Aunt Prudence would be home about four, Michael too. Until then she had her father all to herself. She started lunch. She had given a great deal of thought to the menu and the table was laid with a pure linen cloth, glass ware and silver gleaming with the polishing she had given them.

He was to have everything the way it

had been. These last years had to be wiped out, forgotten completely.

He was a long time in the bath. She got worried and crept upstairs, listening outside the door. The subdued splashing reassured her. They probably didn't have baths in prison. Showers, a long line of men, no privacy, warders watching. She shuddered. It was a kind of death to a fastidious man.

He looked better when he came down, more relaxed, less hunted. A small smile flickered when he saw all her efforts. He sat down, tasted his drink appreciatively, opened the box of cigarettes.

She had forgotten a lighter. Neither she nor her aunt smoked. "I'll get a match," she said quickly and searched frantically for a box.

"Everything doesn't have to be perfect," he said gently, when she rushed forward triumphantly. "It's enough to be free, to be with you again."

She touched his hand, turning her head away so that he wouldn't see the rush of tears in her eyes again. "It's been such a long time. I wanted everything to be just the way you liked it."

"And it is. Tell me what you've been doing with yourself. Your aunt tells me you like your job."

"I do now. I was moved out of the typing pool last month. They made me secretary to the personnel manager, Mr. Travis. He's very nice and the job is interesting."

"Does he know why you've taken the day off?"

"No." She had lied about it and was ashamed of herself. She moved away guiltily. "Lunch will be ready in half an hour."

"I think I'll take a short walk while you're busy. Just down the road and back. You don't mind, do you?"

"Of course not. Put your coat on though. It's very cold outside."

"It doesn't matter." His smile was a little forced and she didn't have to think very hard to guess why. He had been the protective one, the one who had fussed over her. She was reversing their roles and he found it galling. She would have to watch herself.

She put the coated veal in the frying pan and went to the window. He was standing at the garden gate, looking in both directions. It was minutes before he moved. What was he afraid of? The police? Did he imagine they were watching him? Surely they wouldn't have the manpower to waste like that.

He was back within twenty minutes, the greyish pallor of his face tinged with blue. She smiled at him and he said, "Thank you."

"For what?"

"For not saying I told you so."

"Oh!" She shook her head and laughed. "Would you like another drink?"

"I'll get it. How about you?"

"No thanks. I've got some wine in the fridge. Will you see to it? I always seem to leave half the cork in the bottle."

"Yes, of course." He was eager to be doing something to help. She wished she could think of something else for him to do.

It was like trying to make conversation with a stranger, only worse because of the closeness that had existed between them.

"What are you going to do now?" she asked when she had removed the plates and brought in the cheese.

"I'll see Miles before I do anything."

"Why?"

He chose a piece of Stilton carefully. "Maybe he'll give me a job."

"But you can't! Not after—"

"I've no pride left, Melody," he interrupted. "None at all."

"But there must be other jobs."

He looked down at his hands then said quietly, "I've dealt in jewels all my life but what kind of people will employ me now? Trust is essential. Miles does know me. I think he'll take me on."

"Oh, I'm sure he will," Melody said bitterly. "He'll enjoy that. He always did resent playing second fiddle to you. I'll bet it was the happiest day of his life when he bought you out. And why did you do that, father? We'd have managed somehow."

"It cleared my debts. It gave me enough to provide for you and Michael. I had no choice. Why didn't you go on to university? You know that was what I wanted for you."

"I couldn't, father. I'm sorry. I just couldn't."

"All right. I understand." The bitterness was on his side now.

"I was earning money. I thought we'd need it. We can go away somewhere and make a fresh start."

"Oh, Melody. Is that what you've been living on? A pipe dream? Wherever we go someone will find out about me. Besides there's Michael. We can't spoil his schooling. Your aunt tells me he's doing very well."

"Yes . . . he has brains." An abundance of them. If only he had a little more understanding, if only he could believe in his father, put himself in his place. She was dreading their meeting and it was

21

far worse than she could ever have anticipated.

He was late. It was almost seven before she heard the click of the latch on the garden gate. She'd been listening out for it, trying not to show the strain.

Aunt Prudence had blithely ignored his absence. She had taken over when she came home, making the afternoon almost one of normality, enlivened by her brother's presence.

Peter relaxed completely under the casual, common-sense approach and when she got up to start dinner he went on listening to a Mahler symphony with Melody curled up in the chair opposite him.

She was out of it like a shot when she heard Michael.

"Now listen to me," she began as he thrust open the back door.

He brushed past her roughly. He was tall for his age, stringy but with the promise of width on his shoulders. He was going to be like his father, big and dark, with the same straight nose and handsome features.

"So you're here," he said, standing at the door of the living-room and staring at his father with hard eyes.

"Yes, I'm here." His father rose slowly to face him, a nerve throbbing at his temple but otherwise very calm.

"We don't want you," Michael cried. "What did you have to come back for? Why didn't you stay where you belong, with all the scum of society?"

"That will be quite enough, Michael," Aunt Prudence said crisply. "If you can't remember your manners, go up to your room and stay there until you do."

"Manners! And what does he know about manners? He ruins our lives, he makes us ashamed of our name. He's a thief. So stupid he couldn't even get away with it. Now everyone will be talking about it again." His face was dead white. "I'll go to my room—and I'll stay there —until he's gone."

He wheeled around and ran up the stairs. The slam of his bedroom door echoed through the house and then there was only the Mahler and an appalled silence.

Melody was the first to recover. She went to her father. "He's very young," she said desperately. "He doesn't mean it. Forgive him."

"He was right. I shouldn't have come here. I knew it all the time." The vein at his temple stood out like a contoured ridge.

"Darling, sit down."

"No, I must go."

"He has to learn," Aunt Prudence said. "If you go, he'll think he can get what he wants any time by throwing a tantrum."

"You'll say anything, both of you. Anything but the truth. You've managed very well without me. You don't need me —and I'll only cause more trouble."

"*I* need you, father." Melody stood very still. "A day hasn't passed without my thinking of you, not one solitary day. You couldn't help being away from us— I understand that—but now . . . you *can* help it now, father. And Michael needs you too. He might not think so but he does. You have to win back his respect and love. Running away from us won't help to achieve that."

"And that's good sense," Aunt Prudence added briskly. "Let's have dinner. I've had quite enough emotion for one day."

"I'm sorry, Prudence. I don't feel like eating. I think I'll take a walk."

"You'll be back?" Melody asked anxiously.

"Yes, I'll be back." He touched her cheek lightly. "And I'll wear my coat this time."

"Melody!" Her aunt called her from the kitchen as her father left the house. She was fumbling in her bag. "Give him that," she whispered, pushing a ten pound note at her. "He probably won't have much money."

"Oh, Aunt Prudence!" Melody hugged her tightly and then ran after her father. "Aunt Prudence sends her compliments," she said, and pressed it into his hand. "Don't get roaring drunk. Remember this is a respectable neighbourhood."

For a moment she thought she'd said the wrong thing again and then he laughed softly. "That's my lovely. I'll behave."

She leaned against the gate watching him. The avenue was well lit but the trees cast deep shadows and there were several cars parked in the roadway. One of them started up, and revving noisily, went off into the darkness right at the end of the avenue.

Her father glanced behind him only once. He was walking at a steady pace. She wondered where he was going. Where *could* he go? Who would give him a welcome? He'd had plenty of friends; he was a gregarious man. But a man with a prison sentence would be diffident about making that first approach after his release, especially after being so deeply hurt by his own son.

She waited until he'd turned the corner. No one was following him. She turned to go into the house and something, some sound, made her look round again. A man had appeared from nowhere. He walked on rubber-soled shoes, a silent figure, the light glinting on hair that seemed as silver as her father's as he walked under the lamplight. But he was young. He moved easily, like an athlete—or a hunter after prey.

A cold shiver of apprehension touched her spine. She took a step after him, then paused. Her father's nervous fears were catching. There was a dog at the man's heels. He was taking it for a walk; a perfectly normal everyday scene.

Shaking her head at herself she went inside again. Aunt Prudence had dished up the food but she didn't eat with her usual healthy appetite. "Where do you think he's gone?" she said after a while.

"I was wondering that too." Melody hadn't much enthusiasm for eating either.

"He'll be all right," Aunt Prudence said, but for once she didn't sound very sure of herself. "I'll take a tray up to Michael and have a talk with him."

"He's thinking of what people will say all the time. As if that matters."

"It's not as simple as that—and don't

be too hard on him, Melody. Remember you wouldn't go back to school at all."

"But—" She met the comprehension in her aunt's eyes and flushed. She was right. She usually was. She hadn't been able to face the girls. It had been near the end of term; it had seemed the noble gesture to say she was getting a job. She had not acknowledged it as an act of cowardice, not even to herself. But if her aunt had guessed, maybe her father had too.

Feeling sick at heart she cleared the table. She hadn't done much to make her father proud of her. She'd not even earned very much money. The Careers' Officer had found her the job. He'd been more concerned with placing her in a firm which provided her with some kind of training. He'd talked a lot about potential and the short-sightedness of going for more money in a dead-end job. She'd listened to him and gone for the job he recommended, junior in one of the big insurance companies. They had a training scheme for their secretarial staff and she had a whole day at school as well as evening classes. After a year she'd been placed in the typing pool and under the close supervision of Mrs. Young, the middle-aged supervisor, she had gradually moved up the scale from copy typist to going out to take dictation and then placings in temporary capacities as secretaries were ill or on holiday.

The personnel placing was a permanent one, her first. She was determined to make a success of it. Consequently it was something of a shock the next morning when she went into the office and found another girl sitting at her desk.

She was late. Lack of sleep and worry about her father had slowed her up. But it was only ten minutes after the normal starting time. Not enough time for Mr. Travis to assume she was taking another day off.

She bounded in to him, her stomach churning. "I'm sorry I'm late but—"

"Never mind that," he interrupted brusquely. He was a small man, dwarfed by his desk.

It was his job to make people feel at ease; he cultivated the free and easy approach. It was ominous, that touch of brusqueness.

"You've been assigned to a new job," he said abruptly. "It's a temporary one —looking after one of the men from our London office. He's making an O and M report and as you've worked in most of the departments at one time or another you'll be a big help to him."

The words came out as if they'd been rehearsed and drilled into him, flat and without intonation.

"Do I have to do it?" she said forlornly. Just as she was getting into this job and liking it. He glanced up quickly but his eyes slid away almost at once.

"I'm afraid so."

"You don't want me to work for you any more?"

That got to him. He said quickly. "I didn't say that. No, that's not so at all. I've been very pleased with your work, Melody and indeed I don't—"

A soft cough interrupted the sudden

spate of words and the earnest fervour was wiped from his face at once.

Melody shot round, startled and embarrassed. She should have guessed someone else was present from Mr. Travis's manner, instead she had made a fool of herself, being so childishly pathetic.

"This is your new boss," Mr. Travis said. "His name is Glenn Hunter."

The man had been leaning casually against the wall with folded arms. He was tall and lean with smooth flaxen coloured hair, dressed unobtrusively in the standard wear for the up and coming insurance executive—dark suit, white shirt, discreet tie—but she wasn't her father's daughter for nothing. The suit had been made by a master at his craft, the shirt was handsewn and the tie was silk.

He came towards her and she took his outstretched hand politely. He had the deepest brown eyes she had ever seen in a man. They contrasted oddly with his hair and held the kind of assurance she always found off putting.

He retained his hold on her hand too. Another thing she disliked in a man. She pulled it away assertively. She had met the predatory male before. She knew how to treat them.

He smiled as if reading her mind. "Melody!" He had a lazy drawl, confident, almost caressing. "An unusual name."

She didn't answer. Every feminine instinct was sharpened to a point of intense awareness. This one was different. He appraised her deliberately, marking her down as a quarry. He wouldn't be easy to brush off. This man was dangerous.

2

"HOW long do you expect to be up here, Mr. Hunter?" she asked in brisk, business-like tones.

"Two or three weeks. A lot depends on you."

She felt the colour rising to her cheeks but she said primly, "I'll try to do my best to make your stay as short as possible."

There was amusement in his voice. Battle had commenced and they both knew it. "That's very nice of you, Melody. Mr. Travis tells me you're not afraid of hard work." He turned to Mr. Travis and thanked him smoothly for his assistance and then he steered Melody out of the room. "I was fixed up with an office yesterday. I'm afraid you'll have to share it with me, space being at a premium here." He took her along the corridor and opened a door at the end. It was a small room and there were two desks in it, one a fairly large one. It didn't allow much space for manoeuvring.

Melody eyed it dubiously.

"I'll be out a fair amount," he said, reading her thoughts again. "I'll need to talk to a lot of people. They're sending a typewriter up from the pool. As soon as it comes I'd like you to make a list of everyone employed here, with a brief rundown of their jobs. You can borrow the files from Mr. Travis. I've already cleared that."

He stepped smoothly back as the door exploded open and a porter staggered in, red-faced and breathing heavily with a battered old Remington in his arms.

Melody stared at it in horror. "A manual!"

"Sorry—there's no plug in this room. You can use one surely?"

"Yes." She swallowed hard. She'd used one at college but it wasn't an experience she wanted to repeat—and not now. She wanted to produce a superlatively splendid job. She had her pride to consider.

"Mrs. Young brought up the paper and carbons she thought you would need. I'll leave it to you. I'll be out most of today." With only a few more words of explanation he was gone, leaving her to stare bleakly at the typewriter.

He didn't reappear until fifteen minutes before she was due to go home. She'd had the worst day of her life. The typewriter couldn't have been used for years; it was heavy and unwieldly and very hard work.

"That's not really very good, is it?" he said, glancing through what she'd done.

She could have cried. Her hands were aching, her arms were aching, and she had a splitting headache.

"It's the best I could do," she said in a low voice. "This machine must be out of the ark." She bit her lip. Bad workmen . . . But he didn't say it.

He sat down at his desk, leafing through her typing. She struggled on, tired and too conscious of his presence to do any more than make a token gesture.

At five to five she started to put her things away. He glanced up. "Oh, I'd be grateful if you could put in some extra time."

"If you mean tonight, I'm sorry. It's out of the question."

"Why?"

"Because if I do any more tonight I'm liable to end up throwing this machine out of the window," she said bleakly. "And besides I'm expected at home."

"You've got a date tonight?"

"No."

He regarded her in silence for a few moments and then he said, "I was given two tickets for a show. It would be a pity to waste them and I can see you've had a rough day. I'll pick you up about seven."

She was flustered. Instinctively, she started to refuse. "I'm sorry—"

"No buts. You'll enjoy yourself." He came over to her desk and picked up the files from which she'd been working. "I'll take these back. Run off home now."

He was gone before she could say a word. She closed her mouth with a conscious effort. She could wait for him to come back but she had a feeling it would be a waste of time trying to argue so she put on her coat and went home.

The scene was a peaceful one of domestic harmony when she got in. Both her father and Aunt Prudence were in the kitchen but her father followed her into the sitting room as she flung herself down on the sofa and asked what kind of day he'd had.

"I went to see Miles," he said. "But he's away all week in Amsterdam, so I had lunch at the Carousel. There was no one I knew there."

Or no one who wanted to know him. The idea that had come to her the night before grew stronger. He needed a friend. Someone outside the family.

"I've had a perfectly ghastly day," she said, and started to tell him all about it.

"And he's coming here tonight?" Aunt Prudence said, not having missed a thing.

"You can tell him I've taken to my bed with a splitting headache. That will teach him to be so high handed."

"I'll do no such thing. You'll go out with him and try to be pleasant for a change. You're too fond of turning people down."

She set a casserole dish on the table with a thump and added darkly, "If you're not careful you'll end up on the shelf like me. I was too particular and look where it got me."

Melody let out a peal of laughter. "You poor old spinster woman. I weep for you. You're so obviously soured and frustrated."

"He sounds a forceful character," her father said reflectively.

"You can give him the paternal third degree. That might make him wilt a bit."

"You'll behave, both of you," Aunt Prudence said sternly. "The poor man is probably lonely—away from his home and friends. We'll show him some real Northern hospitality."

"That kind of man is never lonely—and if by Northern hospitality you're thinking of saving some of that hotpot for him I wouldn't bother."

"The trouble with you, young lady," Aunt Prudence began ominously and then changed her mind. "Go and tell Michael dinner is ready."

"*No*, tell me. What *is* the trouble with me? Go on, don't be shy." Melody was laughing again but her aunt was serious as she measured her reply. "You compare every boy you meet with your father. A fixed ideal is dangerous. You don't go out enough. You're young—you should be enjoying yourself. Why if I'd had your looks I'd have been out every night of the week at your age!"

"You didn't do so badly, Prudence," her brother said raising an eyebrow. "Don't push the girl. She can pick and choose at her leisure."

"Then why doesn't she? You'll wear that blue dress tonight, Melody. And you can use my new perfume."

"Before you go any further, Aunt Prudence, maybe you'd better find out if he's married." She grinned impishly at the consternation on her aunt's face. "He could have a wife and ten children down in London."

"You don't think— But surely he wouldn't have asked a young girl like you to—"

"They do," Melody interrupted. "All the time. Terrible, isn't it?" And she laughed and went upstairs to get Michael.

There was no scene. The talk last night with his aunt had borne fruit. Michael showed his hostility only by his silence, excusing himself as soon as the meal was over.

"He has a lot of homework," Aunt Prudence explained as her brother frowned unhappily. "Now you go and change, Melody. I'll do the dishes."

"He can wait for me."

"I begin to see what your aunt means. I'll help in the kitchen," her father said. "Pride, Melody, is important. Pride in yourself and in your work, but there's false pride too. Give your best. You never know how something will turn out."

"What's the matter with both of you?

I only met the man today. Stop trying to marry me off to him."

"Go and get ready," her aunt commanded. "This isn't the time for a philosophical discussion. Your blue dress, mind."

She had already planned on wearing the blue. It was very simple, very chic, and it fitted like a dream. She was going to look her best, however much she might talk.

The doorbell went before she was quite ready and, by the time she had got downstairs, they had already introduced themselves and Aunt Prudence was asking Glenn if he would like some coffee.

"That would be very nice," he said. His eyes looked almost coal black in the electric light. "Do sit down." Aunt Prudence was unusually flustered.

Melody said sardonically, "Don't fuss. I'll get it." She and her father already had cups but there were another two laid ready on the kitchen table. Her aunt's best Spode. "It would serve you right if I dropped it," she muttered in her aunt's ear as she refilled her cup. "More coffee, father?"

"Yes, I think I will."

She poured one out for herself and sat perched on the arm of her father's chair. Her aunt was asking Glenn where his home was.

"I have a cottage in Surrey but I travel a lot in my job." He stirred his coffee reflectively. "It's a lonely life, mainly a hotel existence for me, but when I do go down into the country I really relax."

"So you've no family?" Aunt Prudence said, flashing a look of triumph at Melody. Mission accomplished. The way was clear.

Melody nearly choked on her coffee.

"No, I've no family."

Melody felt he was very carefully not looking in her direction.

"You'd be very welcome to have dinner here one night," Aunt Prudence said. "Saturday perhaps. That's always the worst night to be on your own, isn't it? Perhaps you could let Melody know."

"I can tell you right now, Miss Ford,

that I would be delighted to accept. It really is extremely kind of you."

He was a different person again, Melody reflected. Polite, almost deferential, certainly exceedingly amiable. There was no sign of the forceful magnetism that had put poor Mr. Travis in such a tizzy.

After his second cup of coffee Glenn put his cup down and glanced at his watch. "Time we were going, Melody."

She went meekly for her coat without a word, conscious of her father watching her.

"Enjoy yourself," Aunt Prudence said, coming to the door to see them out.

"I'll make sure that she does," Glenn said. He glanced back at her father, hovering in the background. "Don't worry about her, sir."

"What makes you think he was worrying?" Melody asked as he held open the door of the car for her.

"Wasn't he? He was sizing me up pretty thoroughly."

"I'm surprised you noticed. You were

so busy being charming to Aunt Prudence."

"She's a nice person."

"I'm sure she thinks the same about you. I've a brother too but he'll be a little harder to win over."

"Harder than his sister?"

"It's a debatable point."

"What do I have to do to make a hit with you?"

She cleared her throat nervously. "Would you mind stopping at the end of the road? I'd like to make a phone call."

"Don't you have a telephone at home?"

"Yes." Her tone was meant to freeze any further questions before he started but he said unperturbably, "I'm not sure I want to be party to any kind of deceit."

"Don't worry," she said coldly. "I'm not conducting a clandestine affair or breaking the law in any way."

He glanced down at her quizzically but she wasn't going to say any more, and after a second's hesitation he pulled into the kerb.

Natalie Galbreith was in the directory.

Melody felt that was a good sign. It could so easily have been an unlisted number. Nevertheless, she felt nervous as she dialled. She had met Natalie once but it hadn't been a momentous meeting, merely a token introduction as she had waited in the shop for her father.

She recognised the voice at once though. The husky tones were unmistakable.

Melody ran her tongue over her lips and said jerkily, "Mrs. Galbreith? This is Melody Ford, Peter Ford's daughter. I'd like to speak to you about my father if I may. D—do you remember him?"

There was a short silence at the other end. A pregnant silence. Melody pressed the receiver against her ear. Her hands were growing wet and sticky. Then Natalie said slowly, "Yes, I remember him."

Melody took a deep breath and pressed on. "You were good friends once. Could you ring him—just to say hello and make him feel that someone is glad he is no longer in prison."

"When did he—when was he released?"

"Yesterday."

"I see." There was another silence, longer this time. Melody said desperately, "He didn't take your jewels, Mrs. Galbreith. He was innocent. He should never have gone to prison. And now he has no friends, no money, no job, nothing. Even his own son doesn't want to know him."

"It's all right, Melody. Don't get upset. I'm not trying to think of a tactful way of saying I don't want anything to do with your father. On the contrary . . . But if I telephone he'll guess you had something to do with it and it won't have the same effect. Hasn't your house been sold and you're living with your aunt?"

"Yes."

"Then I think an accidental meeting would be better, don't you? Let me see . . . the Carousel used to be a favourite lunching place for him, didn't it?"

"He went there today."

46

"Well, make sure he's there tomorrow. I'll be there about one o'clock."

"One o'clock," Melody repeated. "Thank you, Mrs. Galbreith. Thank you very much."

Natalie laughed. "Who knows. I may end up thanking you. Good-bye, Melody."

Melody leaned against the side of the booth, feeling wobbly with relief. Natalie had sounded almost pleased that she had called.

She jumped as the door of the phone booth was pulled open and Glenn said, "A satisfactory talk?"

"You were listening?" she demanded suspiciously.

"I had that in mind," he told her blandly. "But you must have picked the only phone booth in this country that's not been hit by vandals and you were reasonably soundproofed. You didn't answer my question. What do I have to do to make a hit with you?"

"You could start by minding your own business," she snapped.

"But you are very much my business —for the next two weeks at least. Shall I try to do something about that typewriter for you?"

"Unless you want your stay to stretch to a month it might be a very good idea."

"Ah," he said reflectively. "A month . . . now that's not the way to get things moving. Supposing I like the idea of extending my stay here?"

She dropped her eyes at once and turned to the car. "Hadn't we better be moving? We're going to be late."

He laughed but dropped the subject and they made it to their seats as the lights were dimming.

The play was a well written thriller that held people intent. Melody enjoyed it.

As they filed out into the foyer Glenn glanced at his watch. "We've time for a drink I think."

She said at once, "If you don't mind I'd prefer to go home. It's been a long and hard day."

His mouth twitched but he didn't try to persuade her, only when they reached the door of her aunt's house he said, "You're going to invite me for coffee, aren't you? I see the lights are still on downstairs so I presume you'll be properly chaperoned."

She faced him, the key poised in her hand. "You needn't think I'm afraid of you in any way."

"What makes you say that?"

She regarded him gravely.

"It seems to me that you like to make people nervous of you," she said finally. "Why was Mr. Travis so uneasy?"

"A lot of people are uneasy when I'm around. It's the nature of the job. Don't you worry about it though, I rarely recommend redundancies amongst the secretarial staff."

"I'm not worried," she said flatly.

"Then why mention it?"

She stared at him. It was hard to make out his expression although there was more than enough light from the house to illuminate his face. Those dark, dark eyes, impenetrable and remote. She had a feeling he wasn't merely seeing her as a person. There was something else, something more complex.

She had a sudden certainty that she would never understand this man however well she might get to know him. Maybe it *was* the nature of his job, maybe it was because he was met with suspicion and fear wherever he was sent.

Every man knows himself to be fallible, vulnerable in some area of his job. They would try to cover up, hide their discrepancies—and to be good at his own job he would have to be something of a detective, never allowing a liking for a man, or woman, to influence the decision he had to make. A man alone. He had to be.

But not outside work. That was why he had been different with her Father and Aunt Prudence. There was no reason to erect a force field with them. And with her? Maybe she had imagined that moment in the office, or rather misinterpreted it. He wasn't dangerous, not to her. He was only an ordinary man. She could handle him. And then she wasn't so sure. He held her chin firmly within the palm of his hand and bent his head and kissed her before taking the key from her unresisting hand and opening the door.

She charged past him like a clumsy elephant fleeing from danger, humiliated and angered by the response that had risen up in her.

It had hardly been a kiss, a mere brushing of the lips and yet it was as if the world had turned a somersault.

Both her Father and Aunt Prudence were still up. Unable to contain their impatience to learn how she had got on, she thought resentfully and rushed into the kitchen before they could take a guess by seeing her face. "Coffee, everyone?"

"Not for me," her father called out but Aunt Prudence said she would like one, asking Glenn what the play had been like.

He was sitting in his chair as if he were a regular visitor when Melody entered with the tray.

She avoided his eyes, and her father's, and handed round the coffee.

51

"Not having one yourself?" Aunt Prudence said in surprise.

"No, I'm off to bed now." She had quite enough to keep her awake already. The look on her aunt's face told her she was being rude but she couldn't help herself. She couldn't remain in the same room as Glenn, not now. She said good-night and went upstairs.

It was another half hour before Glenn left. She watched him from her window as he walked down the path and it was as though she had watched him before.

He turned, his eyes going straight to her bedroom. He couldn't possibly see her. She was certain of that, but instinctively she drew back and just then Aunt Prudence entered the room and switched on the light and she was as sharply outlined as a figure in a spotlight.

She brought the curtains together with such force the rod bounced with the strain. "Did you have to do that?"

Aunt Prudence blinked, her eyes widening, but she said mildly enough,

"I'm sorry. I knew you weren't asleep. Did you have a nice time?"

"Yes." She bounded into bed and pulled the covers up to her chin. "Goodnight again, Aunt Prudence."

"It's like that, is it?" Her aunt sounded amused. "All right, I can take a hint. Sleep well." She clicked the light off and softly closed the door behind her.

Melody was out of bed in a flash and over at the window again. She opened the curtain a bare crack but Glenn had gone.

She leaned on the sill, prey to feelings she had never experienced before. Why should the touch of a man's lips fill her with panic? She had been kissed before.

She got back into bed, annoyed with herself. She wouldn't behave like that with him again.

Her father was late in getting up the next day. She knocked on his door just before she was due to leave and asked him if he could take her to lunch. "I want to talk to you," she said.

"Is it about that Hunter fellow?"

She hesitated and then nodded. It was

as good a reason as any, and besides she would like to talk about Glenn. Her father was a man of the world. His advice would be welcome. "Twelve-thirty," she said. "At the Carousel," and whisked away before he could suggest an alternative.

She was early. Glenn had appeared first thing in the morning and then vanished again. No mention had been made of the evening before. He was crisp and business-like and she equally so, her guard well up.

She ordered a dry sherry and was sipping it slowly when her father arrived.

The Carousel catered for the people with money to burn; the fashionable, the smart. He looked out of place in the suit that no longer fitted him well and where once he might have carried it off with his supreme self-confidence, his present apologetic hangdog air was enough to make any waiter lead him to the furthest corner where no one could see him.

Melody smiled brightly to cover her dismay. Natalie couldn't see him like this, not her father. Pity wasn't what he wanted.

"You order," she said as the waiter brought the outsize menus over. "Let it be like it used to be. Remember when it used to be my big treat. Remember my sixteenth birthday?" She watched the lines around his mouth ease and his eyes brighten as she talked. They had been good times. He had loved to take her out.

As she prodded at his memory and brought a thousand things back to mind, something of his old manner returned and he forgot his self-consciousness, ordering with a certainty that surprised the waiter.

They were half-way through the meal when Natalie appeared.

Melody saw her first. She glanced up and blinked. Natalie was a small vibrant woman of great charm and intense femininity, whose constantly losing battle against her ever increasing flesh in no way influenced her choice of clothes. Discretion wasn't a word recognised in her vocabulary but where most people of her diminutive height and less than diminutive build would have looked slightly ridiculous in what she chose to wear, Natalie always contrived to look magnificent.

She came slowly towards them, causing the usual stir that always attended her appearance. Her dress was of Thai silk and a mink coat was draped casually around her shoulders.

She had never been poor but the Galbreith money had lifted her out of the class of the ordinary well-to-do where normal rules applied. She was a personality, an eccentric almost. Her name had been linked with many men since her husband's death but she had never married again.

Melody lowered her head. It was Natalie's move.

She stopped by their table and it seemed an age before her father glanced up, and then he froze in sudden stillness.

"Hello, Peter," Natalie said softly.

He rose to his feet automatically but the nervousness, the apprehensive uncertainty, returned like a mantle to his shoulders, dragging him down and locking his tongue.

Melody felt every sense in her body aching for him, crying out his need, and perhaps Natalie felt it. She smiled. "I'd like to join you if I may, or are old friends taboo now that you've returned to us? What was it like in there? Ghastly I expect."

A chair appeared like magic, a fresh place was laid. She continued to talk, taking such attention for granted, and gradually the colour returned to Peter Ford's face and he found his tongue. "You've not changed one bit, Natalie," he said in half unwilling admiration.

"Where are your eyes? Look at my figure. I put on a pound if I as much as look at a cream cake but you—you must have lost a couple of stones at least. All that stodge they give you too. It's rank injustice. Why didn't you answer my letters, Peter? I wrote to you—three times."

The change in tone was very revealing. Melody lowered her eyes quickly. She had begun to suspect last night but now she was sure. Natalie had been in love with her father.

He said stiffly, "I could never answer them. You should have understood that."

"No. I didn't understand. I don't understand now. You are a proud man, Peter Ford. Too proud for your own good. You didn't take my jewels. Do you think I ever imagined you did? Everything I had could have been yours. You had only to say the word. You knew that. And you chose to think that an obstacle. If I'd been living on ten pounds a week you wouldn't have hesitated, would you? *Would you?*"

"Natalie!" Peter Ford exclaimed weakly.

"Oh, not in front of your daughter! Dear me, no. It *is* Melody, isn't it?" Natalie turned her brilliant eyes on Melody. "I happened to love your father very deeply. He had some misguided notion that I had too much money. Would that worry you?"

"Er—" She gulped, swallowing air.

"I don't know. If I were a man perhaps . . ."

"Yes, yes. A man has to be the provider always. A foolish idea. Should I give all my money away? And now . . . now I don't suppose you can pay for my lunch so you won't even want to talk to me."

It was back to her father again. He wilted under the bombastic power and then as she carried on in the same strain his mouth began to twitch. "All right, Natalie. You've made your point. I was a fool, I still am a fool—but you're like a breath of fresh air and I love you for it. Stay for lunch. I think I can afford it."

He was all right. Relief made Melody feel almost lightheaded. She put down her knife and fork. "If you don't mind, father, I think I'd better get back to the office. I only have an hour and it's almost up."

"Oh, but . . . we didn't get around to discussing that young man of yours."

"He's not mine, and it will keep."

"A young man?" Natalie regarded her

with speculative eyes. "Yes . . . I can see you've done some growing up this last couple of years. Bring him down for the weekend. I'm having a welcome-back party for your father at the cottage."

"Oh, but—"

"No, you can't—"

Father and daughter spoke simultaneously but Natalie ignored them both. "It's all arranged," she said, bestowing a carelessly dazzling smile on each in turn. "A little bird told me you were out, Peter. I didn't come entirely by chance to this restaurant. I was looking for you. Now Melody, I'll expect you some time tomorrow afternoon. I'll send the car for you—all of you, your aunt and brother too. I'm not listening to any refusals and don't glower at me like that, Peter. This is a time when you need your friends. Now run along, Melody. Leave me to talk some sense into your father."

Melody hesitated. Natalie had turned up trumps with a vengeance but there was good reason to be apprehensive about a mass confrontation with all his old friends. She put her hand on his shoulder. Maybe it was better this way though. "I'll see you later," she said. "Don't argue too much. I think we should go."

He covered her hand with his own. He was smiling faintly. "Glenn Hunter too?"

"Well . . . He's not—"

"Only he's over by the door and I think he's coming over."

She straightened up slowly. It couldn't be coincidence. He must have overheard something of that telephone call with Natalie. Enough to guess she was meeting someone. She felt a burning resentment start to kindle in her stomach. What she did was no concern of his. Glenn Hunter had to be put in his place . . . right now. And she was going to do it before Natalie saddled her with him for the weekend.

And then she went cold all over. If that phone call was mentioned her father would know she had been "the little bird". Everything would be spoiled. He would think Natalie was only being kind, responding to the pleas of his own daughter, and all his new found confidence would crumble. She had to keep Glenn Hunter quiet—whatever the cost.

3

HE was at their table before she could gather her wits together and head him off but she rushed into speech at once. "I'm afraid your dinner date with us tomorrow will have to be postponed, Mr. Hunter. We've just bumped into an old friend of my father's and she is insisting that we stay the weekend with her. Mrs. Galbreith, this is Glenn Hunter. He is spending a couple of weeks up here to do an O and M report in the company. Mr. Hunter—Mrs. Galbreith."

Natalie extended her hand. "How do you do, Mr. Hunter. I'm sorry to interfere with your plans for the weekend but I've assured Melody you'd be very welcome to come along too."

Melody rushed headlong again. "I'm sure he's got better things to do, Mrs. Galbreith, and I must get back to the office. Are you coming too, Mr. Hunter? My father and Mrs. Galbreith have got a lot to catch up on. It was such a surprise to meet again here."

It was clumsy but he couldn't put his foot in it now. Not unintentionally.

Glenn smiled at her and then at Natalie. "A tactful child, is she not? I don't have anything better to do, Mrs. Galbreith. In fact, I'd be delighted to accept your invitation."

Natalie smiled, appraising him with approval. Her voice was almost a purr. "I'll look forward to making your acquaintance then."

"And come to lunch with us," her father added. "To console Prudence for not being able to cook dinner for you."

So he had made up his mind. There was to be no argument with Natalie.

Glenn smilingly accepted that invitation as well and then allowed himself to be borne off by Melody.

She waited until they were outside the restaurant before she spoke again and then she said ominously, "Don't tell me you arrived there by chance. You wanted to know who I was meeting, didn't you?"

"I was curious. It's an insatiable disease with me." He walked swiftly, not only blatantly admitting his curiosity but wanting to know more. "So you arranged a meeting between your father and Mrs. Galbreith and you were frightened of your father finding out. Why? It appears to be a very interesting situation."

"What do you mean by that?" she panted breathlessly.

He glanced down, slowed his pace. "Am I going too fast for you?"

"I think you are."

"Don't worry. I got the message. I won't breathe a word—provided of course, that you stop trying to show me to the door. What have you got against me? And why the Mr. Hunter bit? It was Glenn last night."

"It was not. I didn't address you by name at all."

"Perhaps not aloud." He smiled. "What's it all about, Melody? Maybe I can help."

She was tempted—for just a moment. But how could he help? And supposing she told him and he felt bound to tell someone in the company? They wouldn't be very keen on having the daughter of an ex-convict in their employ. They might even decide to sack her.

She said stiffly, "You can help by not mentioning the phone call I made last night."

His eyes hardened, the sympathy leaving his face. "Very well," he said curtly and strode the rest of the way back to the office in silence.

They met Mr. Travis as they entered the building. He muttered some kind of greeting and stood like a robot beside them in the lift.

Glenn had nodded carelessly. He didn't speak seemingly unaware of the effect he had on Mr. Travis, who normally would have been chirping happily about something or other.

Melody said warmly, "It's a lovely day, Mr. Travis. Isn't it nice to see the sun again?"

"Yes, Melody. Yes." He stared straight ahead, his gaze resolutely turned away from them both and when the lift door opened he bounded away as if he were escaping from someone infected with the plague.

"You left the files out," Glenn said. "If you leave the room for any length of time I think you'd better see that they are returned to Mr. Travis."

"I'm sorry. Does he have them now?"

"No. I put them in your drawer."

She slanted a look at him wondering if he'd done that in order not to advertise her shortcoming to her regular boss. Probably not. He would be putting her in her place.

He didn't stay in the office very long and still hadn't returned by five o'clock. She took along the files to the personnel office. The girl had gone and Mr. Travis was just shrugging into his overcoat.

Melody smiled at him a little tentatively and went over to the cabinet where the files were kept. As she dropped them into their respective slots Mr. Travis cleared his throat. "Er, Melody . . . ?"

"Yes?"

"You're not getting too friendly with this Glenn Hunter, are you?"

"I wouldn't say that."

He looked acutely uncomfortable. His fingers jerked in his collar as if it had grown too tight.

"You're a nice girl," he said. "And you're very trusting. Be on your guard with him."

She smiled reassuringly. "Don't worry, Mr. Travis. I'm no Judas. I won't tell him a thing he could use against anyone."

"No, no," he said in strangled tones. "I'm not worried about that. It's you. You don't—" He froze as the outer door opened and said rapidly, "Have a nice weekend, Melody. I'll see you on Monday," and he was gone, leaving her staring after him in astonishment.

"Goodnight, Travis." It was Glenn who had entered. He came through to the inner office. "I thought I'd find you here. I'll give you a lift home, Melody."

"You needn't bother."

"It's on my way." He paused and added in a different tone. "Is anything the matter?"

"No." She banished the astonishment from her face. She'd see Mr. Travis on Monday. She'd find out what it was that was bothering him so much about Glenn Hunter. "Where are you staying? I'd have thought you'd have chosen one of the big hotels in the centre of town."

"It goes to show you should never make hasty judgements. I'm at the Arundel—only round the corner from you. It's a family concern, much less soul destroying than the big chains."

She knew it vaguely, although she had never been inside. It was on the main road, close to the bus stop where she waited each morning. "How did you get to hear of that?"

"When you travel as much as I do you get to know about hotels." He smiled at her quizzically, "If you want to continue this cross examination let's do it on the way home. It's very bad for the morale to be last in the building on a Friday evening."

"Oh yes . . . I'll get my coat." Flushing slightly, she ran down the corridor. Had it sounded suspicious? What *had* Mr. Travis been going to tell her before Glenn had so untimely interrupted.

She kept thinking about it all the way home but could come to no satisfactory conclusion. He could think Glenn was too good looking, that he was maybe the type of man who ruined a girl's reputation, maybe that she would get hurt. But that didn't explain his nervousness or the way he had frozen up when he'd heard the office door go. Though that could relate to his job, his wish not to antagonise the man. She gave up on it. She could wait until Monday. Two days weren't going to make any difference.

"What time do you have lunch?" Glenn asked as he pulled up.

"Around one," she said reluctantly.

"I'll see you tomorrow then." He leaned across and opened the door for her. "Goodnight, Melody."

She got out and slammed the door. "And goodnight to you too," she muttered under her breath, stomping up the path, annoyed with herself for the abrupt lurch of her heart as he almost touched her. What was the matter with her? She didn't want him around. She'd shown him that. He'd forced himself on her. But as she let herself in she knew very well she didn't think him capable of telling her father about that phone call. A man would have to be without heart and conscience to do that.

She found her father had not yet returned so she had the job of breaking the news about the change of plans for the weekend.

Michael immediately declared that he wasn't going, that nothing on earth would make him.

Melody regarded him dispassionately. "You're going if I have to drag you by the hair and what's more you're going to be pleasant about it. Don't you realise what you're doing to father? Have you ever been blamed for something you

71

didn't do? You must have been. Think of that burning sense of resentment, the hurt and the anger. If you'd been in trouble at school do you think father would just have disowned you and wanted nothing more to do with you? He would have moved heaven and earth to find out who was really to blame. He would never have wavered in his belief of you. And you—you— You can't even be decent to him, you're so busy wallowing in your own self-pity."

"That's not fair," Michael cried, his face pale with anger.

"Fair! Do you imagine this weekend is going to be a picnic? Have you any idea of the amount of courage it will take for him to meet people again. The least we can do is give him a feeling of solidarity. There'll be some there only too ready to turn the knife and he knows it."

Michael turned an agonised glance at Aunt Prudence. "She's right, Michael," she said quietly.

"But I can't go. I can't."

"No one is going to force you." His

father had let himself in by the back door and was standing listening. "You're old enough to make your own decisions now." He met his son's eyes steadily. "I know how you feel and I can't blame you. The jury found me guilty. What right have I to demand you believe them wrong?"

Michael stared at his father. A scarlet flush had overlaid the paleness. He swallowed visibly and Melody held her breath. "Would you *swear* to me that you didn't take those jewels?"

"I do swear it. I'm no thief, Michael."

Michael's hands went to his side, clenched and taut, and then he turned abruptly and went out of the room.

Melody made a movement to follow him but her aunt stayed her with an upraised hand. "Let him think it out," she said quietly and she looked at her brother. "Perhaps you should have done that at the beginning of all this. Blind faith is not always enough."

He sat down heavily. "He was a child then. Now he seems an adult young stranger. I've failed my children, Prudence."

"He has a long way to go yet before he starts thinking like an adult. Melody, see if the potatoes are ready yet, will you?"

She couldn't have signified her intention more clearly. Melody closed the door on them. They were close those two, closer than she had imagined. She started to cream the potatoes wondering what Michael would do now. She couldn't start to make a guess. Maybe she'd failed him too. He was the younger. She could have helped him instead of hating him for what she considered his defection.

He didn't come down for dinner and there was no sign of him the next morning.

"He's eaten though," Aunt Prudence said, eyeing the loaf of bread which looked as if it had been attacked with a hacksaw.

"What will we do if he doesn't come back by lunch time?"

"He'll be back," Aunt Prudence said

serenely. "You'll see. What would you like me to give Glenn for lunch?"

"I don't care. How about tripe and onions?"

Her aunt laughed. "You'd be the first to protest if I put that on the table. Why don't you admit it, Melody? He's a very attractive man. Playing hard to get doesn't always work."

"I'm not playing hard to get. I'm not ——Oh you!" she flushed. "I'll get the shopping."

"Don't take too long. We have a lot to do this morning."

Michael returned just after twelve. He edged into the kitchen. There were dark smudges of exhaustion under his eyes. He didn't look as if he'd slept much. "I've decided to come with you," he announced.

"Good." Aunt Prudence wasn't going to make a big thing out of it but Melody said warmly, "I'm so glad Michael. And I'm sorry if I've said some rotten things to you in the past. You've got more guts

75

than I have. I ran away from other people. I just couldn't face them."

"And you're still running," Aunt Prudence said on a note of surprise. "I've just realised it. That's why you won't make any friends."

"That's not so."

"*Melody*!"

She couldn't meet her aunt's eyes.

"What are you afraid of? That they won't want to know you if they find out about your father?"

"I don't care what other people think."

"You're a liar," Michael said bluntly. "You're ashamed of him. The same as me."

"No. No, it's not like that." She glanced apprehensively at the door. Her father had gone for another of his walks but he would be back at any moment. She would have died rather than allow him to think she was ashamed of him.

Oh, she was worse than Michael. Much, much worse.

"I bet they don't know at work, do

they? I bet you've never told a soul," Michael went on relentlessly.

"Do you think they would have employed me if they knew? I had to keep it quiet."

"Oh, Melody." Her aunt shook her head tiredly. "You can't run away for ever. Do you realise Glenn is likely to find out this weekend?"

"I don't care if he does. I don't care about him. I don't care—" Her voice broke and it was her turn to rush away.

She threw herself down on her bed. But she couldn't cry. She couldn't go down and face her father with reddened eyes and a puffed face. She wasn't ashamed of him. She wasn't, she wasn't.

"Melody?" It was Michael.

"Go away."

"No." He came into the room. "I'm sorry. I didn't realise . . . I didn't know. You were always so self-contained, so scornful of me."

"Covering up my own inadequacies you mean?" she said bitterly. "I'm not ashamed of father. I'm ashamed of myself. I couldn't bear people to look at me with pity, or scorn, or distrust."

"I know how you feel." He sat down on the edge of the bed. "Believe me I know. I'm ashamed of myself too. And if he didn't do it . . ."

"Oh, he didn't." She sat up then. "I've never doubted that—not for an instant."

Michael got up and went over to the window. "He never lied to us," he said in a low voice. "He always used to say it was a coward's way out."

"I remember." Melody's voice was equally low.

"If he didn't do it, who did?"

"I don't know. The jewels have never turned up. When they do maybe the truth will come out then."

"It won't turn him back to the man he was though, will it? It gave me an awful shock when I saw him."

"Prison must change a man." Melody said gently. "Especially a man like father." There had been a tremor in Michael's voice that didn't escape her.

"He's lost his confidence. We can help to give that back to him at least."

"Yes." His voice steadied. "And you help me and I'll help you. Who is this Glenn?"

She told him briefly and he said, "Aunt Prudence likes him, doesn't she? She's not often wrong about a person."

"She doesn't know him."

"And you do?"

"No. I don't know him either."

"But you like him?"

"He—" She broke off. Heavens above! Michael was only a child after all. How could she explain the feeling Glenn Hunter aroused in her. "I've never met a man like him before," she said carefully. "He makes me feel that he can read my mind and it frightens me."

"Why?"

"I suppose I'm afraid of being hurt."

"But why should you be hurt?"

"Oh Michael, I can't explain." She thought of Mr. Travis, dithering and nervous. "He's in the kind of job where he has had to be ruthless and hard. I

79

don't think people's feelings matter very much to him."

"Will he see you're fired if he finds out about father?"

"It's not that what worries me. Well, perhaps it does a little," she added, forcing herself to be quite truthful. "But he's a man who doesn't follow the ordinary rules. He might not think that important. He might . . ." She paused. He might use it to his own advantage. Would he do that? *Could* he do that? Why *was* he being so persistent? "Do you think I'm attractive?" she said inconsequentially.

Michael blinked and then said with brotherly frankness, "I can't see it myself but one or two of the chaps think you're a smasher."

"Hurrah for them." She got up off the bed and went over to the mirror.

"Blokes go for blondes," Michael added ingenuously.

"Umm." She pushed a stray tendril of hair into place. "*He's* blond too. But his eyes are as dark as very black coffee. He looks at me and . . ."

"There's the bell. I bet that's him now. You'd better do something to your face. You don't look very glam. I'll answer the door."

"You'll do no such thing." Never mind what she looked like. She wasn't going to risk Michael imparting some frank brotherly revelations while she wasn't there.

He had a head start but she caught him up at the bottom of the stairs.

"You'll behave yourself," she hissed, hauling him back by the collar and pushing past him, but even as she opened the door she reflected that Glenn had at least served one good purpose that day. He took Michael's mind off his father and eased the tension.

Lunch was actually a pleasant occasion and if Glenn noticed the constraint between father and son he gave no sign of it. Michael was trying, really making the effort, but it was hard for him. Far easier to talk to Glenn who seemed to

81

know all about cars from the year dot. Michael was mad on cars.

The one that arrived to take them to Natalie's made his eyes widen. It might not be one of the racy ones he favoured but he wasn't too young to be able to resist the gratification of going in a chauffer-driven Rolls.

"We'll follow you," Glenn said to Melody's father.

"There's plenty of room," Aunt Prudence said. She had never met Natalie and she was nervous but she was glancing up and down the road hoping at least one or two of the neighbours would see this grand departure. "You can leave your car here. It will be quite safe."

"I'm the independent type," Glenn said cheerfully. "And I can't bear anyone else to be in the driving seat when I'm in a car."

He picked up Melody's suitcase. "Is this all you have?"

It was a large case and she'd filled it, prepared for every contingency. She met his amusement belligerently. "It's the only case I possess." A battered case too. She'd once had a set of matching Revelation cases in bright red leather. It had been a wrench to part with those.

He raised an eyebrow. "Upset about not travelling in style in the Rolls?"

"No, of course not."

"They why so grouchy?"

"I am not grouchy." She marched to the car and stood waiting for him to open it. It was a black saloon, anonymous and discreet and looking more than a little battered, not at all what she would have expected him to drive. "Is this your own car or one you've hired while you're up here?"

"It's mine." He closed the boot and unlocked the door for her.

"I'd have expected you to have a Jag or a Jensen at least."

"Oh?" His mouth twitched. "Why?"

"Well, you do like power, don't you?"

He went round and got in, switching on the ignition before he said, "That's a paralysing observation. Jumping to conclusions again?"

"Do you enjoy your job?" she asked curiously.

"Most of the time."

"Doesn't it bother you to have people regarding you with suspicion?"

"It surprises me on occasion. You, for instance. You've been perfectly charming for the last hour or so and now we're alone you're all prickly again."

"I am not."

He slanted a glance down at her, smiling a little. He didn't carry it further but his silence was provocative.

After a moment she said crossly, "Well, all right. What do you expect when you force yourself on me and are so high-handed? You didn't even ask if I wanted to drive with you."

"So it *is* the Rolls."

"No, it is not. And if you're not careful you're going to lose them." The Rolls was sweeping ahead and another car edged in between them.

"Never mind. I have the address. So you think I'm forcing myself on you?"

"Don't you consider you are?"

84

"I think you'd be very disappointed if I were to back out now and show no further interest in you."

She sat up straight in her seat, quivering with indignation. "It would be a matter of complete indifference to me."

"Indeed?" He smiled again. His complete imperturbability was infuriating.

She didn't speak to him again for the rest of the journey.

He glanced down at her once or twice but made no attempt to get her to talk. It was something of a disappointment. She had a feeling he was laughing at her.

He drove well, without any hesitation, even though the Rolls had long gone from sight, and it was a little after five when they reached the village of Kensham where Natalie had her cottage.

It was at the end of a narrow driveway cut through a mass of scrub and spindly trees.

"How do you know this is it?" Melody demanded uneasily. She could see the house, four square, tall and sombre looking, like an old Victorian workhouse, and as far removed from a cottage as a Mandarin from a Chinese coolie.

"Now what's running through your mind now? Allow me a modicum of common sense. I phoned Mrs. Galbreith last night and her directions were very clear."

"What did you telephone her for?" Melody demanded in astonishment.

"I always like to know where I am going."

She stared at him and then decided to pass on that one. "It's not at all what I expected," she said flatly, transferring her gaze to the house.

"Things rarely are." He regarded the house thoughtfully. There was no sign of the Rolls or any other car but the drive went round the house.

He followed it, stopping before a double garage with a forecourt of macadam. The chauffeur was waiting there and he waved Glenn into the garage.

Melody got out of the car. Steps at the side of the house led down to the lake. It was even more sombre looking than the house, the high rushes and overhanging trees adding to the gloom and imparting an air that seemed sinister and mysterious.

She shivered suddenly, feeling she wasn't going to enjoy this weekend but inside the house all was warmth and light and Natalie couldn't have given them a kinder welcome.

The others were already in front of a blazing log fire tucking into afternoon tea with toasted crumpets and sandwiches and cakestands overflowing with all kinds of pastries and confectionery.

"You'll want to go up to your rooms first, I expect," Natalie said and led the way upstairs, dropping Melody off first in a demure little room and taking Glenn further along the corridor.

He was next door but one. Natalie returned almost at once. "I wanted a little talk with you," she said, shutting the door behind her. "Did your father say anything to you last night?"

"About this weekend?" Melody shook her head.

"He's nervous." Natalie walked about the room. She seemed nervous herself. "I want everything to go off well. About two dozen people are coming. I thought a buffet dinner would be wiser—more informal. They are a mixed bunch. People we used to meet fairly frequently before . . . well— He doesn't like to talk about it, does he? I thought it best to be blunt but now I'm not so sure."

"Mrs. Galbreith, I think you could get away with murder. Don't worry about being tactful. He won't recognise you." She coloured, realising what she'd said. "I'm sorry. I didn't mean to sound rude."

Natalie laughed. "I think I know what you mean. And call me Natalie, please. You might as well. Cards on the table. I mean to marry your father. I don't know how on earth I'm going to do it but this time I won't let him get away. Do you have any objection?"

"Well . . ." Melody didn't know what to say. "Er, no. Not if you make him happy."

"Oh, I'll do that never fear—once I get

my hands on him. Have you any idea how I can go about it?" There was something very appealing about her as she stood there. A woman of the world, exotic and glamorous, experienced in life, with everything anyone would think a woman could want, and she was asking Melody for help.

Melody said softly, "He won't marry you while everyone thinks he's a thief."

"No. I've thought of that. The odds are far greater than they were before. Is he going to try to get a job?"

"He's going to ask Miles for one."

"Oh!" Natalie bit her lip. "Miles . . ." She turned, going over to the windows and drawing the curtains against the deepening dusk. "I never liked Miles. Do you think he could have had anything to do with the theft?"

"I don't know," Melody said honestly. "He didn't appear to have the opportunity."

"Well . . . if your father does go back there we'll have to do something about that. He'd be a perfect scapegoat for anything happening again." She turned abruptly. "I'll have to leave you or your father might start putting two and two together. I don't want that to happen. Not until he's better adjusted."

She left Melody to wash her hands before joining them for tea. The guests started to arrive well before eight and Melody was on tenterhooks for the next hour.

Natalie, however, had it well in hand. She rarely left her father's side, bright as a peacock in a long flowing kaftan, chattering vivaciously and ever ready to turn the conversation with an adroitness that filled Melody with admiration.

She saw her father laughing again, talking easily, her aunt relaxing at the sight and joining in a conversation with a group of people, Michael in tow, silent and all eyes at his first adult party. Glenn was talking to a very sultry blonde. He'd hardly spoken to her all evening.

She went to refill her glass. There seemed to be an unlimited supply of almost every drink in existence and the buffet table was groaning under the weight of all the food.

She eyed it appreciatively but the gargantuan tea had destroyed her appetite —or something had. She kept her back to the room, determined not to give Glenn any reason to think she minded being deserted by him.

"You're Ford's girl, aren't you?" The voice made her jump. There was a rasping sneer in it that put her on the defensive at once. She turned slowly. He was a big heavy man with a sagging chin and pouched face but he still had the remnants of what must have once been an attractive masculinity.

"I'm Melody Ford, yes," she admitted warily.

His eyes ran over her deliberately. She had on her blue dress again. It was the only one equal to the occasion. "So Natalie's taken you all under her wing," he said nastily. "Isn't that wonderful? Giving us orders to come and be nice to the man who got away with her jewels."

"You'd better watch your tongue," Melody said in a low voice.

"Or else what? Natalie will smack my bottom and send me home for being a naughty boy? She wants to open her eyes. Look at him. He thinks he's got it made. A free meal ticket for the rest of his life. It makes me want to puke."

Melody turned away from him. She was trembling with anger.

"Hold it, hold it," he said. "I've not finished with you yet. I've got a proposition to make. You're his darling daughter, aren't you? I'll bet you could find out where he's stashed the jewels. How about it? Fifty-fifty! He'll sit on them for ever with Natalie in his pocket."

"You must be out of your mind to say something like that to me," she said furiously. "My father was innocent."

He gave an ugly laugh. "Don't be silly. You look like a sensible girl. His eyes ran over the blue dress again. "One who appreciates the finer things of life. I could show you how to live." He leered at her. "What do you say?"

She didn't say anything. She slapped his face, using such force that it sounded like a pistol shot.

All the colour fled from his face and then the impression of her fingers began to stand out like a red imprint.

She took a step backwards, horrified at what she had done and then she felt real fear as he grabbed her by the shoulders. "Why you little—! I'll teach you—"

She felt the enormous strength of him, smelt his breath, stale with whisky and cigarettes, saw the hot fury in his eyes and then he was shaking her, his fingers digging cruelly into her flesh and she couldn't even find the breath to scream.

4

HE was plucked off her as if an eagle had swooped down and carried off his prey.

Melody staggered back, her hands going to her throat. It was Glenn who had come to her rescue. He said coldly, "After you've apologised to Miss Ford I think you'd better leave."

The man swayed on his feet and then lunged at Glenn. It seemed impossible for him to miss but Glenn side-stepped ducking under the flaying fists and delivering a hard punch right in the middle of the soft belly of fat so temptingly exposed. The man folded up with a cry like a punctured windbag abruptly cut short as Glenn took advantage of his unguarded chin and hit him with his left hand, sending him shooting back across the floor to land heavily on his back. He was out cold even before his head snapped hard against the carpet.

There was a silence that was absolute. The guests stood frozen. Her father stood there like a man in a trance and Natalie's mouth had gone slack in horrified alarm.

Michael was the first to recover. His eyes were shining. He said enthusiastically, "Boy! You sure can hit."

Someone laughed, the group shifted and came to life and Natalie hurried forward, throwing her arms around Melody. "Darling! Don't look like that. He was as drunk as a kite."

"Who is he?" Her voice was wobbly and uncertain.

"His name is Walter Hartley. But forget about it. I should never have asked him."

Glenn was bending over him. Her father walked slowly across the floor. "I am in your debt. That was something I should have done."

"I was nearer." Glenn dismissed the matter. "He's coming round."

Hartley groaned, his head going from

side to side. He stared blankly for a moment, pushing himself up, his eyes going round the room, and then they fastened on Melody and hardened into sharp probes of enmity. He got to his feet clumsily.

"You are no longer welcome in this house," Natalie said. "Please leave." She stepped in front of Melody to shield her, facing Hartley with her head flung back and her eyes blazing.

"Who do you think you're protecting?" Hartley sneered. "The daughter of a jailbird! You're sinking low, Natalie. I never thought to see the day when you'd be mooning over such a man."

"One more word out of you," Glenn said very softly, "and you'll be *carried* out of this house."

Hartley turned, measuring Glenn with cold deliberation. "You had a lucky punch. Don't press your luck, boy."

"Get out," her father said in sudden anger. "Get out of this house."

"Playing the master already!" Hartley's lips turned down in a grimacing sneer.

"I'll go. Who wants to stay to watch the spectacle of a deluded fool with more money than sense playing right into your hands! Your daughter had better watch out though. I've not finished with her yet. She's going to find out that—"

He never finished his sentence. Glenn moved first but her father was only a second behind and they frogmarched Hartley out of the room before he could do anything to stop them.

"Well!" Natalie said, expelling her breath in a long sigh. "I would never have believed it."

"If you don't mind, Natalie," Melody said unsteadily. "I think I'll go to my room."

"You do as you please, my dear. Only forget about Walter Hartley. He had ideas about marrying me. That was the real reason for that scene." She patted Melody kindly. "I'll send Jean up with a hot drink for you."

"No, don't bother." She managed to smile at Natalie and went to her room but it was suddenly close and stuffy and she had a longing to be outside in the fresh air where she could breathe freely.

She picked up her coat and slipped downstairs. It wouldn't have surprised Melody to find everyone making a hurried departure but Natalie was too good a hostess to allow that to happen.

She went outside and round to the back of the house. There was a little path running by the edge of the lake and she followed it slowly, her shoes sinking in the muddy stretches, her legs scraped by the heavy undergrowth.

She stumbled over an exposed root but went on walking until she came to a little wooden jetty standing out over the edge of the lake. The wood was rotten, she felt a plank give as she walked on it, but she went on and sat down on the edge, staring out across the lake. It stretched for about half a mile, narrowing to a ribbon that gleamed dully under the moonless sky. The wind had dropped and the surface was no longer ruffled but lay like a huge pool of ink, black and dark, reflecting nothing.

She became conscious of small sounds in the undergrowth; a cheep of some nightbird, the croaking of a frog, and of the intense cold that came up from the jetty, numbing her senses and cloaking her in a mantle of ice. That was how it should be; no pain, no feeling. Impossible to be hurt when she felt like this.

And then a voice came out of the darkness behind her and she knew she would have to be dead to be without feeling. "What are you trying to do? Catch pneumonia?"

"Leave me alone," she said dully. Glenn was the last person she wanted to talk to.

"Not on your life."

He came on to the jetty and his foot went through the rotten planking. He swore and she turned quickly, "Are you hurt?"

"No." He pulled his foot out gingerly. "You could have broken an ankle out here and no one any the wiser until morning. This jetty is falling apart."

"Here, let me help you." She went

towards him but their combined weight was too much for the strained timbers. There was an ominous creak and then Glenn had got hold of her, throwing her with him to the safety of the ground. She landed heavily, all the breath knocked out of her but all she was conscious of was Glenn's arms around her and his face close to hers.

He held her without moving and she too was motionless and then his lips were on hers and nothing else mattered.

But then he had pushed her away, he stood up and his voice was cold, remote. "We'd better get back."

"I love you," she cried. "I love you." Her voice reflected all the glory and wonder of it.

"You don't know what you're saying."

She understood then, the coldness penetrated, only this time it was worse than before. She got slowly to her feet. "The daughter of a jailbird, that's it, isn't it? I'm no good for a man with ambition." And turning like a mortally wounded animal she ran back along the path.

The same exposed root that had tripped her before caught her again and she went sprawling. She beat her hands against the hard earth, the tears falling bitterly down her face, twisting away from him, fighting as he tried to help her up.

"Stop it," he said sternly. "Stop it."

She went limp, numbed by the pain as he unwittingly shook her on the bruises Hartley had made. He set her on her feet. "It's not that," he said. "It's not that at all." He was gentle, his hands no longer hard and demanding. "You're very young, you've got your life before you."

"It's all right. I understand," she said tonelessly.

"Look at me." He caught her by the chin, forcing her eyes to meet his. The shadows of the night softened the planes of his face, accentuating the hollows and making him a strange and somehow alien figure. "You don't understand at all," he said. "You know nothing about me."

"I could learn."

"Oh, you'll learn," he said in a low voice. "Come on back to the house before you freeze to death." He put his arm around her, half carrying her, and saw her to the door of her bedroom. "Sleep well," he said, and touched her cheek, holding the moment. "I'm not a nice character," he said. "But I don't want to hurt you."

She lay in bed staring at the ceiling. Sleep well! She didn't feel as if she would ever sleep again but some time during the night she fell into a deep slumber and was wakened by one of Natalie's maids bringing in a coffee tray.

She sat up slowly, wincing as the movement brought pain. Her neck felt stiff and she felt lethargic and lazy.

"It snowed during the night," the maid said, setting the tray down and going over to pull back the curtains.

Light flooded into the room, blinding at first. The whole countryside was covered in a blanket of startling whiteness, which sparkled under the early rays of the morning sun.

Melody caught her breath, slipping out of bed to get a better view. The trees were stark black shapes on the landscape, the branches decorated with a two-inch edging of frosting. Nothing moved, all was frozen into stillness. It was incredibly beautiful.

"Breakfast is between eight and nine," the maid said. "But Mrs. Galbreith wondered if you might like it in your room."

"No. I'll be down."

She poured a cup of coffee, sipping it slowly. It was a new world, a new day. She'd been upset yesterday, her nerves on edge . . . and then that scene with Hartley. But it was no excuse for the way she had acted with Glenn, hurling those words at him just because he had kissed her.

She stirred uncomfortably at the memory. She'd made a fool of herself and he'd been kind. Kind! Some of the coffee slopped over the edge of the cup. His words were burned into her brain. She was young. *Very* young. But he hadn't thought of her youth that first time in the office. No. And he hadn't been thinking of that when he kissed her.

She closed her eyes, re-living that moment again. There had been magic there and she would create it again—whatever he thought, however much his conscience pricked him. His conscience! Why should he care about hurting her? He must have hurt many girls in his time. How old was he? Thirty-two, thirty-three?—and not married.

She traced the curve of her cheek pensively, resting her fingers on her lips. If a conquest was all he was after he wouldn't have pushed her away at that point. Something had stopped him. And it wasn't the thought of her father. A man out for what he could get would consider that something to take advantage of.

She went down to breakfast considerably cheered by that thought. If he cared enough to worry about her being hurt, he could care some more. She would make him care.

Her aunt was the only one in the breakfast room. "The others have gone out to test the snow," she informed Melody. "Anyone would think it was a hundred-year phenomenon. Natalie isn't up yet. It must have been nearly four in the morning before the last guest went home."

"Everything went with a swing then?" Melody lifted the covers on the dishes over the warming stand. There was a tempting variety again and this time she did full justice to it.

Her aunt looked at her loaded plate with raised eyebrows. "I take it you're feeling fit and well."

"Not first thing but the sight of all that snow lifted my spirits."

"I looked in on you last night but you were sleeping like a baby."

It was Melody's turn to raise her eyebrows. "You must have been rather late yourself then. I didn't get to sleep for ages."

"Oh, I was having a ball," her aunt admitted blithely. "And I think your father enjoyed himself too. Except for that horrible scene it would have been a perfect evening. Why *did* you slap that man's face, Melody?"

"He asked for it," she said shortly.

Her aunt pursed her lips and reached for the marmalade. "I once slapped a man's face," she said pensively. "It was a very satisfying gesture but not perhaps advisable in a room full of other people."

"In the circumstances I was rather glad we weren't alone."

"Yes. A nasty piece of work." Her aunt spread the marmalade lavishly across her toast. "I think Natalie thought he might do something for your father. He's in the diamond trade."

"He could never have worked for a man like that," Melody said emphatically. "He wanted me to find out where father had hidden the jewels. He promised me half of the proceeds."

"No!" Her aunt stared at her aghast.

Melody went on with her breakfast. She was wondering if Glenn had returned to the party and how she could phrase the question without her aunt drawing any conclusions when her father appeared.

"They've got too much energy for me," he said with a sigh, flopping down into a chair. "Is there any coffee left?"

"Plenty." His sister poured him a cup and he took it from her gratefully. "Thanks. Mornin' Melody. How do you feel?"

"Fine."

"No repercussions?"

"A few bruises," she said lightly, safe in the thought that he couldn't see. The area around her throat was black and blue but she'd covered it with a polo-necked sweater.

"I suppose I can guess something of what he said to you."

She lied at once. "It was nothing to do with you. He was so full of his own conceit he thought he'd only to say the word and I'd fall into his arms. I had to make it very plain to him that I wouldn't touch him with a barge pole."

"A brave try." Her father's lips twisted. "What really made you so angry?"

"Honestly, father, you're becoming so

107

self-centred you think everything revolves around you." She tried to make a joke of it. "Take a good look at me. I'm young and beautiful. Can you wonder that an old goat like that fancied his chances?"

"Old goat," her aunt snorted, as anxious as Melody to turn the subject. "I suppose anyone over twenty-five is old to you?"

"Well, er, not quite."

"Oh? You'll settle for an extended range in exceptional circumstances? How old is Glenn?"

A blush spread painfully over her face. Trust her aunt not to miss a trick. "I'm sure I don't know."

"He's a good man," her father said quietly.

"Because he knocked down Hartley? Maybe you think I should feel flattered —but if he hadn't deserted me for that emaciated blonde it would never have happened. Did he join her again when I went to bed?"

It was out. No subtlety, no hiding the

fact that she cared. She could have bitten her tongue out.

Her father sat up sharply in his chair, staring at her as if seeing her in an entirely new light.

Her aunt said, "So it has happened. I thought it would." There was no satisfaction in her voice, rather resignation and regret.

"Isn't that what you wanted?" Melody cried.

"I don't know." Her aunt looked away from her. "I wanted you to have a good time, to be aware of yourself and the fact that men existed. You have a lot to learn, Melody. Glenn is older than you and I don't think he has any plans for settling down."

"I don't care about that."

"Don't you?" Her aunt shook her head. "I know better. Your mother was just the same."

"What do you mean?"

"She means that some people stay true to their first love and never know any other," her father said in a low voice.

"Your mother was your age when she first met me. She never looked at anyone else."

"She never got the chance," her aunt put in tartly. "Don't misunderstand me, Melody. I liked your mother. In fact, I was very fond of her, but first love is not always the best. Enjoy yourself with Glenn. Have fun. He's the type who knows how to treat a girl and you can learn a lot from him. But, please, please, don't give your heart to him without thinking of tomorrow. You want a good marriage, children, the kind of security that has nothing to do with money."

"I thought you liked Glenn."

"I do. He's charming, attractive and knows exactly what to say to make a good impression, but somehow he gives me the feeling that I'm an analytical specimen. A prod here, a poke there, and I react as anticipated. Oh, I know it sounds silly, Melody, but I'm afraid for you. He's too good to be true."

"And there you see why my dear sister has never married," her father said dryly.

"She can never believe in anyone but herself. There has to be trust in this world or no one would survive. For what it's worth, I like him. If you want him go right ahead. He's taken the hook."

"Why do you say that?"

"Maybe you weren't watching him last night. He might have appeared to be taken up with that blonde you described so disparagingly but he hardly took his eyes off you. How do you think he acted so promptly when you were in trouble? And he went after you like a scalded cat when he found you weren't in your room. Oh, don't look so confused. Do you think we just dismissed the matter when we saw Hartley off the premises?"

"A telephone call for you, Mr. Ford." One of the maids put her head round the door. "You can take it in the library if you wish."

"Who is it?"

"A Mr. Mathieson."

"Miles!" He sprang to his feet, all tiredness forgotten. "How did he know I was here?"

"The social grapevine," her aunt commented, leaning back reflectively. "What's the betting that some little bird has been on to tell him all about last night?"

"He's not the social type," Melody said. "They pointed that out at the trial. He stays at home with his wife and doesn't go in for the kind of entertaining that costs money."

"I'll lay you odds on anything you like that he's going to offer your father a job." Her eyes were half closed. "Someone has told him about Natalie's efforts—that goes without saying. I expect he's missed the business your father brought in. Custom doesn't flourish without word of mouth, my dear. Friends and friends of friends are what count, not a sign on the door. Your father had a great many friends."

"How did he meet my mother?" Melody said irrelevantly.

Her aunt's eyes snapped open at once, understanding glittered in their depths. "He was a very attractive man—like

Glenn. He went his own way, discarding as lightly as he chose. We never thought he'd marry. He liked the gay life too much, the variety, the spice of conquest, and then he met your mother. She wasn't like his other girls. She had no family and she worked in the shop. I think he fell in love with her almost right away. They were married within three months."

"I can hardly remember her," Melody said with regret. "I can't even picture her in my mind—only the photographs. When she died the gap she left didn't hurt for very long."

"That was because of your father. He turned to you. Sometimes I feel it was a mistake." Her aunt examined her nails critically. "No man can mourn for ever. It's not in his nature."

"If you're trying to lead up to the fact that he'll marry Natalie, don't waste your breath," Melody said with some amusement. "Natalie has warned me already that she intends to get him to the altar by hook or by crook."

"And you don't mind? Obviously not.

113

I would have thought— But never mind. You lacked a mother in your formative years, when you had the most need of one. I've tried to guide you and Michael in the best way I could but I had the feeling I failed with you. I'm sorry I pushed Glenn at you. I love you, Melody. I don't want you to be hurt."

"That's what Glenn said. That he didn't want to hurt me, I mean."

"Oh?" Her aunt looked at once hopeful and alert. "What made him say that?"

"I don't know."

"Maybe—" She broke off as her brother bounded into the room. "Miles wants me to start work on Monday," he announced. "He's being very generous. I didn't even have to ask him. He suggested it himself."

"And you're going?" Melody said with a sinking of her heart. She knew the answer already. Her father's enthusiasm told its own tale.

"I can't afford to turn it down. Miles is all right. He believes in me. Everything will be just as it was before."

"Except that you'll be working for him. Your father started that business. How can you bear to do it?"

"Oh, that's unimportant." Her father brushed it aside. New energy was running through his body.

Melody's heart sank lower and lower. Her aunt was nodding her head in approval. Did she think that getting a job was all important? That her father's self-respect could not be gained in any other way?

And when she heard that Walter Hartley had been the one to tell Miles where her father was staying her misgivings grew even stronger. A scapegoat Natalie had suggested. Could she be right?

She excused herself as soon as she had finished eating. She could bear it no longer.

Monday! That was tomorrow. She had to wake Natalie. She would do something about it. She went upstairs, opening each door along the corridor until the exotic

115

scent of Natalie's perfume met her and told her she had the right room.

She slipped inside and switched on the light. Natalie was sprawled diagonally across a big double bed. Her long hair had been released from the pins that held it in her chic hairstyles and she looked younger and very vulnerable without her makeup. The light didn't disturb her. She slept on peacefully.

Melody hesitated. It seemed a shame to disturb her. And then she thought ruthlessly that Natalie could catch up on her sleep later. She had all the time in the world. Her father had not.

She touched her shoulder, gently at first and then with more force. Natalie moaned and turned over away from her. "Go away," she muttered indistinctly.

"Natalie. It's important. Miles has just phoned. He's offered father a job."

Natalie sat up sharply, instantly awake. "How did he know you were here?"

"Hartley called him this morning."

"*Hartley*! Why?"

116

"Apparently he wanted to know if he and father were still associated."

"But why?" Natalie demanded again in bewilderment. "I don't understand."

"Maybe he made Miles the same offer he made me. Fifty per cent of the proceeds if he could find out where father had hidden the jewels."

"The proceeds? The insurance reward for their recovery you mean?"

"No, I do not."

"But Hartley's a wealthy man. You must be mistaken."

Melody didn't answer and after a moment Natalie said, "Did you tell your father of this?"

"No. I said he'd made a pass at me. He didn't believe me though."

Natalie pressed a switch on an elaborate intercom and asked for coffee to be sent up. "For two," she said.

"I've only just had breakfast," Melody protested.

"One can always drink coffee." She ran her fingers through her hair. "He was drunk last night. He couldn't have known what he was saying."

"I don't suppose he was drunk this morning when he rang Miles."

"Well, we don't know the reason for that. No, I'm sorry, Melody. Hartley proved himself a rotter last night but I can't believe he's in need of money so badly that he'd go against the law. He has too much to lose. I suppose your father jumped at the job."

"Yes."

"He would," Natalie said bitterly. She glanced up as the maid came into the room. "Thank you, Jean. Put it down there, would you."

She got out of bed and pulled on a bright coloured robe. There was nothing of the frills and flounces in Natalie's room. It was sleek and functional, a place to work and relax as well as sleep. Crossing to a rosewood writing desk, she opened it and went unerringly to one of the cubbyholes, producing a fat leather address book. She flipped through it rapidly and then reached for the phone.

"I'm phoning my solicitor," she said. "He won't take very kindly to being disturbed at home but I'll get him to set up an appointment tomorrow with someone who's used to this kind of thing."

Melody had no idea what she meant, not until she went on talking crisply into the phone and it began to fall into place. She wanted her solicitor to recommend a detective agency. Someone discreet and very efficient. Her father was to have a watchdog, a shield, someone to cover him for any eventuality.

"We can't tell your father what we're doing, of course," she said authoritatively as she came off the phone. "It would weaken the credibility of any statement if it came to the point of a police matter. Besides, your father might not understand."

"I don't think he would," Melody said weakly. She felt she needed that coffee after all.

Natalie poured it out absently. "I think the secretary would be best," she murmured. "Although I'd prefer a man. How many people work in the shop?"

"Four or five in the back, a couple of girls and Miss Teddington—she's the one who does the secretarial work. That was in my father's time of course. Things might have changed." Melody sat down. She wasn't so sure this was such a good idea. Her father would be furious if he found out. Apart from anything else the cost was sure to be astronomical.

"Well, I leave that part of it to them," Natalie decided. "I want your father covered every moment he is in that shop."

"What do you think is going to happen," Melody asked faintly.

"I don't like Miles Mathieson," Natalie said firmly, "and his offer of a job to your father is very suspicious. If anything else goes missing the police will automatically think your father had something to do with it." She sat smoking, her eyes narrowed. "Maybe we could set something up, lay a trap . . . a consignment of jewels that a thief couldn't resist. *The* thief. Maybe it's not too late to clear your father. A camera set to take pictures whenever the safe is opened . . . That should prove it conclusively."

Melody felt a stirring in her blood. It might work. It was certainly worth trying.

"Well," Natalie said abruptly. "I'll see what the detective has to say. He'll know what can be done. Run along, Melody. I want to think this out properly and get it quite clear in my mind. And not a word to anyone."

"No." Melody put her cup down on the tray and went along to her room.

She took another look at the snow. It would be nice to join Glenn and Michael but snow was about the one thing she hadn't prepared for in her suitcase. Her boots were at home.

Chained to the house she went in search of the library and curled up with a book for the remainder of the morning.

They left soon after lunch. Her father was worried about the condition of the roads. It was not unusual for the village to be cut off for days when the wind piled up the snow in huge impassable drifts on the steep roads between the hills. Natalie travelled back with them. She wasn't risking being snow-bound either.

Glenn had come in with Michael just before lunch. They had made a circular tour of the lake and walked for miles.

"It's fantastic," Michael said. "All that snow and ours the only footsteps. You are really isolated here, Natalie. Doesn't it worry you?"

Natalie laughed. "Not at all. I have every comfort." Which was the understatement of the year. It was the most luxurious home Melody had ever been in.

She looked back at it as she waited for Glenn to get in his car. He had made no suggestion that she travel back with him and she was taking no chances that he would go without her.

The snow had softened the facade but even so it still presented a grim and unprepossessing appearance. Like a prison, she thought and shivered.

Glenn slid into his seat and started the engine. "Cold?"

She said abruptly. "Are you going to tell anyone at work about my father being in prison?"

"Why should I do that?" His tone was completely colourless.

"You might feel it your duty."

"I like your father," he said.

"He didn't do it, you know."

Glenn said nothing.

"He didn't. Truly he didn't." She had to get some response out of him but again he failed to reply, merely glancing down at her.

"We're going to prove it," she said loudly. "You'll see. *Everyone* will see."

"Oh?"

"Yes. Natalie is hiring a firm of detectives. They—" Oh Lord! She couldn't even keep her mouth shut for a few hours. "Don't tell anyone please," she begged. "My father knows nothing about it and it won't work if anyone else got to know."

"What won't work?"

She stared miserably out of the window, imagining what Natalie would think of her if she knew what she was doing, but the damage was done. She might as well tell him the rest, "You *will* promise not to tell anyone," she entreated when she'd finished. "*Please.*"

"You can trust me," he said shortly. "Anyway I'm going back to London tomorrow."

She felt as if a ton weight had fallen over her head.

She stared at him blankly. It was minutes before she could speak. "But why?"

"I think it's best."

"Because of last night?"

He didn't answer.

She said desperately, "I won't embarrass you if that's what you're thinking. You can't go away. The job's not finished yet."

"Someone else can carry on."

She opened her handbag, fumbling for her handkerchief. She wasn't going to cry or make another scene. She blew her nose hard.

"You're running away," she said flatly.

"What are you afraid will happen if you stay? And if you tell me again that you don't want to hurt me I'll scream. As far as I'm concerned the damage is done but I'm not going to make a song and dance about it. It wasn't your fault. It just happened."

"What would you say if I told you it didn't just happen? That I made it happen. Deliberately."

She blinked, uncertain for a moment, and then determined to be reasonable about it. "I suppose that's the aim of most men when they start dating a girl but if that's the case why go away now? I know —don't say it. You've discovered I'm a 'nice girl'."

"Aren't you?"

"Certainly I am. And I think you're a nice character yourself despite your denial of it. If you had no conscience we wouldn't be having this conversation now."

"You see what you want to see."

"Maybe. All I ask is that you don't go away on my account. Finish the job first and then it won't be a black mark against you in the company."

He drove in silence for a few miles. It had started to snow again; the drifts were piling up against the hedges. The Rolls was nowhere in sight and there was very little traffic in the road.

He jammed his foot on the brakes with a muttered imprecation as a man loomed up out of the snow waving a red flag. Winding down the window he asked curtly what was wrong.

The man walked towards them taking his time and ducking his head down to peer at Glenn through the window. "A little difficulty ahead, sir," he said. "They're trying to clear it now." His eyes flickered across to Melody. "It's a Rolls. Skidded clear across the road and collided with a lorry."

Melody gasped, her limbs turning to water. "A Rolls!"

Glenn said sharply. "Is anyone hurt?"

"'Fraid so. An ambulance is on the way." The man's face was pinched and frozen, his nose a ruddy beacon.

"Who—?" She was afraid to ask. Her father? Michael? Aunt Prudence? Natalie?

"Stay here, Melody. I'll find out." Glenn got out of the car.

"I'm coming too."

The man strode over and caught her by the arm. "Better not, Miss. It's a nasty sight."

She tried to pull free. Glenn was walking rapidly and in a moment had turned around the bend and vanished from sight. "I have to see," she cried. "My family was in that car."

"Wait." The grip on her arm was like a vice.

She said angrily. "You're hurting me."

He didn't slacken his grip, if anything he tightened it, and she looked up at him. His eyes were cold, without a speck of sympathy in them.

"Let me go," she demanded.

"Sure," the man said laconically.

A car was coming round the bend but instead of releasing her, he caught hold of her bodily and lifted her up as it came abreast. A door in the back was opened and she was flung inside to land heavily half across the seat.

The man got in beside her and a second later the car was accelerating.

"What do you think you're doing?" She picked herself up. She was shaking with anger and alarm.

The man sat stolidly in the corner, watching her with a measure of speculation in his cold grey eyes. "You be a good girl and nothing will happen to you," he said.

"Who are you? W—what do you want?"

"We reckon your daddy loves you— that he'll fork out those jewels for your safe return."

He got out a cigarette waving the match in front of her. "Start praying, little girl. Because we mean business."

He smiled and then blew it out with a deliberation that suggested menace.

She shrank back in her own corner. "B—but he didn't take them," she stammered. "He can't give them to you."

"You'd better be wrong, lovey. Type,

don't you? Hard to do that with a few fingers missing." He laughed at her expression. "We've never kidnapped a girl before. I reckon it might be fun. What do you say, Les?"

Melody glanced at the driver. He was staring at her through the driving mirror with furtive little eyes.

"Fun," he said in a high-pitched nasally voice and then he giggled.

The sound turned Melody's blood to ice. She closed her eyes. She had to get away. She had to. There wouldn't be much left to live for before they finally had to acknowledge that any attempt to make her father surrender the jewels would be fruitless.

5

THE car sped through the snow. Melody tried to instil some courage in herself. She had to be on the alert, ready for the first opportunity to escape. She tried to watch where they were going but the signposts were half obliterated by the snow and the car was going much too fast.

"I suppose the tale of the accident was a lie," she said dully. At least that was something to be thankful for.

"Course it was a lie. Neat job, eh? No violence. Everything pat. We stopped the Rolls but let her go on when you weren't in it. Had another story ready for them."

"What did you do to Glenn—to my friend?"

"Nothing." He regarded her with bland innocence.

"Never hurt no one unless need be.

He's probably still walking round the bends wondering where the pile up is."

Les coughed. "I wouldn't bet on that, Eddy," he said, adjusting his mirror. "Black saloon, coming up fast."

"Lose it then," the man called Eddy said irritably, turning around to watch through the back window. "Can't be our friend. I snatched his key."

"It's his car."

"I don't believe it. That heap of his didn't look as if it would go above thirty."

"It's his, I tell you. You should have done more than take the key."

"How was I to guess he'd have a souped-up engine. Look at him. Just look at him." His voice rose in alarm.

Melody almost had her nose glued to the window.

Glenn was gaining, slowly but surely, disappearing for a moment when they rounded a bend but bursting into sight again with the certainty of Nemesis, the snow spraying up from the wheels in powerful jets.

Eddy leaned forward, grabbing Les by the shoulder. "Can't you go faster?"

"Not on this road; not in this snow. You want to crash?"

"If we mess this up we might as well be dead. He's going faster, ain't he?"

"Get your hands off me." Les jerked his shoulder free and the car skidded across the road out of control for a heart-wrenching second.

"Holy mackerel!" Eddy yelped. He sat back in his seat, sweat pinpricking his face. "Don't do that again."

"You think I did it for kicks?" Les was hunched right over the wheel. He took the next bend too fast and the tyres shrieked in protest but then they were on the straight and the road was running with true Roman precision.

"Now . . ." Les said, and he put his foot hard down. The distance between the two cars increased and then Glenn had straightened up and he was coming like a bomb.

Eddy began to swear, horribly and monotonously.

"He's got us," Les ejaculated, but all of a sudden Glenn started to drop back, the gap between the two cars lengthened and Eddy slowed in his cursing. "He's bust his engine," he said in half incredulous disbelief. "I knew it. That old crate couldn't stand much of that."

Melody stared in despair as the black saloon seemed to trundle to a standstill. The snow was easing off and it remained in sight for a long time, going smaller and smaller until it resembled nothing more than a big black beetle.

Eddy got out his handkerchief and mopped his face. "I don't mind admitting I was worried there," he said unnecessarily.

Melody sank back in her corner. Why couldn't Glenn have had a decent car? She could have cried.

The road began to bend again but Les took it steadily, confident they were now safe from pursuit. He was heading for the bleak desolation of the moorland hills and as they climbed higher and higher the ground started to drop away at one side, bordered by linked white posts that were almost invisible against the snow.

Melody began to feel very cold. Les dropped more speed until the car was almost at a crawl. He turned on what must have been nothing more than a cart track. She saw a ruin of a house; windows broken, a door on its hinges, half the roof missing.

"Your new address," Eddy said with a smirk. "But don't worry, we've fixed up a nice little room for you. All mod cons and little friends to keep you company. You can think of what you're going to write to your father."

He pulled her out of the car as Les switched off the ignition. "This way."

It had been a farmhouse. The outbuildings were almost non existent but Les turned the car into the remains of what had been a barn and hurried after them, stepping carefully between the broken bits of rubble deceptively hidden beneath the piled snow.

He was a small man, thin and wiry. Eddy dwarfed him completely and yet of the two Melody felt Les was the more dangerous. It was the way he looked at her, with a kind of gloating eagerness. "We deserve a drink after that," he said, his eyes running over her body in a kind of eager anticipation.

"Later. We'll get our guest settled first and then report in." Eddy marched her into what had been the kitchen and lifted a trap door set in the stone floor. "Down you go."

"No." She flinched back. A clammy smell rose; damp, decay, mould and something worse, something putrid and evil.

"Get down there." He thrust her impatiently before him and she stumbled and fell down a flight of stone steps. The trap door banged over her head and she was in complete darkness.

She lay petrified. She felt she'd broken both legs at least and there were rustlings around her, little scurrying noises. Something ran over her foot.

She screamed, and broken bones notwithstanding, made it up to the top of the steps faster than it had taken to fall down them. "Let me out. Please let me out. Don't leave me here." She banged on the trap door frantically and heard Les giggle.

"Please," she begged. "Please."

They weren't going to let her out. Not yet. She sat down as high up on the steps as she could. Maybe she'd not broken any bones but she was bleeding. She could feel the trickle of it on her legs. She wondered desperately what she was going to do. She'd not even got her bag. If she'd picked it up she'd have had her little pocket torch and a nail file. Lipstick too. Maybe she could have done something with that. Write a message or something. Her mind went round and around in circles. What did other people do when they were locked up? They didn't just sit around and cry.

She felt in the pockets of her coat. She had a Kleenex, that was all. One solitary Kleenex. What good was that? She blew her nose on it dolefully. She could be exploring the cellar but down below were those ominous squeaks and rustles. Mice, she told herself. Not rats. Please God, not rats.

She started up as the trap was lifted but it was only Eddy to hand her a storm lantern. "Have a light," he said cheerfully and banged the trap down again.

They *were* rats; sleek and lean with hot red eyes. She stamped her feet and they were gone in a flash but after a few minutes they started to slink back again, watching her with wary intentness, as if waiting for her first mistake.

She fought to keep calm. There was a camp bed covered by an old grey blanket, a bucket, a jug of water, some tins of beans and new potatoes. A tin opener. She grabbed it. It was a weapon of some sort.

The cellar was large. It must have extended under the whole length of the house. She started a tour of inspection, stamping her feet down noisily and holding the lantern high above her head.

Rubble was piled all over the place and

the bright eyes of the rats observed her from a million nooks and crannies.

She couldn't stay here, not for a night. She thought of sleeping on that bed, the rats running over her body, and shuddered.

There had to be another exit, one larger than that trap door. With all this storage space they wouldn't have limited the size of things to be brought into the cellar. Or perhaps they would. It might have been intended as a wine cellar. She went round the walls, hope flaring as she came to a pile of coal. They wouldn't have dropped that through the kitchen floor.

She climbed up it, slipping and sliding as it fell away beneath her. There was a chute. And there was a wide hatch cover at the top. She thrust her shoulder against it and there was a scattering of snow and half an inch of daylight before the coal scattered beneath her and she went sliding down to the floor of the cellar again.

It took five more attempts before she discovered the bolt that was holding it down. It worked on a lever/pulley system located within easy reach from the floor of the cellar.

She leaned hard on the ancient mechanism and wearily climbed the coal once more to push again at the hatch cover.

This time it gave, squeaking and protesting every inch of the way, to fall the last foot with an immense clatter.

She didn't wait for them to come out and investigate. She shot across to the barn to come skidding to a halt. There was no sign of the car. Bang went her hope of making a quick getaway.

She looked back at the farmhouse. There was no sign of life, not even a glimmer of light.

She sat down heavily, all the strength gone from her limbs. They had left her. She could have been eaten alive by those rats. Now how was she to get home from this outlandish place without a car?

Something moved in the shadows of the failing light. A man came out of the farmhouse. She was flat on her stomach before she took her next breath. They hadn't both gone. One had remained. Eddy? It was too tall for Les. He'd have taken the car. Gone to report. At Eddy's insistence? He wouldn't have parked the car in the barn if he'd known he was moving out right away. But Eddy was the type who got scared easily. He was scared of the man they were working for. What had he said? They were as good as dead if they messed it up?

The thought made her squeeze harder against the ground. With such an incentive they wouldn't take kindly to her escape.

It wasn't Eddy. Not bulky enough. And Eddy wouldn't move with such cat-like mobility. She ducked her head down as he turned and stared in her direction. Why couldn't the dark come faster? And then she heard her name called softly.

She raised her head incredulously. "Glenn!"

"Melody?" He sounded uncertain and she scrambled to her feet, half crying in relief. "Glenn! How did you get here?"

"I followed you. What in God's name has happened?"

140

"It's only coal. They locked me in the cellar." She gave her coat an ineffectual beating down but the dust rose in clouds, making her sneeze violently.

"You look like—" He checked himself. "Are you all right?"

"I am now you're here." She stopped trying to make herself look more presentable. It was an impossible task. "I was just wondering how to get home without them catching up with me."

"My car's at the bottom of the hill." He took her arm. "They've gone off somewhere. Fortunately I'd just parked the car in a little spinney or we'd have met head on."

"We thought your car had broken down."

"No. I could have overtaken you but there was a chance you'd have been hurt and as the snow had stopped and the skies looked clear enough I decided I could follow you without them knowing. I thought you'd be safe enough for an hour."

She groaned and he said quickly. "They didn't hurt you?"

"No. I just wish I'd put two and two together. I noticed the snow had stopped too. I could have saved myself an awful lot of wear and tear if I'd waited."

"Oh, I don't know," he said consolingly. "I didn't see any sign of the cellar. I was just beginning to wonder where to start looking next when I saw you."

"You mean you spotted a black heap huddled into the ground."

He started to laugh. "I must admit you're not at all recognisable. They were after the jewels I suppose? A straight swap?"

"Yes." She shivered and he said, "I've got some brandy in the car. Come along."

It burned like liquid fire. Very comforting after the initial shock.

Glenn moved the car back onto the road and turned the headlights on. Night had fallen completely but the snow lightened the ground.

"How did you start your car?" Melody said lazily. The brandy was numbing her

142

senses and making her feel almost drowsy.

"It's easy enough when you know how."

"Oh? And do you have a souped-up engine? They nearly had a fit when it looked as if you were catching up on them."

"It's not exactly what the makers intended for it," he said absently. "I wonder if they intend to return tonight. They'd fixed up a room with a heater and a couple of chairs."

"They said I had to write a letter to my father. I think they've gone to phone someone now. They said something about reporting in."

"I don't expect they'll be long then." He wrenched at the wheel as an arc of light hit the road and then as the car itself rounded the corner, he put his headlights on full beam.

The car seemed to waver for a moment under the glare and then it was behind them and the needle on Glenn's speedometer was rising rapidly. Melody watched nervously out of the side of her eyes. Fifty . . . sixty . . . seventy . . . and then eighty. She stopped watching. Then there was an almighty report and the car slid sideways across the road, going into a gigantic skid.

Glenn fought it coolly, going right into it. Melody closed her eyes. She had a vision of those white posts snapping and being taken down by the weight of the car as it bounced over and over, down to the bottom of the steep incline. She could hardly believe it when they stopped and they were still in one piece—and on the road, pointing in the right direction.

"Burst tyre." Glenn explained briefly. "I'll have to change it."

"Can I help?"

"No. But get out of the car and stand up there by that clump of bushes. At the first sound of an engine I want you down flat. Understood? And whatever happens you don't move."

She said meekly, "All right."

His voice softened. "Take the brandy with you. Keep out the cold."

"Yes, *sir*."

She scrambled up to the clump of bushes he had indicated. It was quite a way from the car. Hugging herself against the cold she stood and watched him. He worked swiftly, his movements sure and economical.

She pushed her sleeve back to peer at her watch but the tiny fingers were undecipherable in the darkness. Had that been Eddy and Les in the car? Glenn had thought so. She stamped her feet and swallowed more of the brandy. They'd have reached the farm by now. Were they looking for her? Would they think she was on foot or connect her with the headlights that had dazzled them not so far away.

She strained her ears, listening for the sound of their return.

Glenn called, "It's okay. You can come on down now."

"They're coming." She had caught the sound, an engine tearing at full speed. She ran towards Glenn and threw herself into her seat as he started the engine. He was only in second gear when the head-lights caught them from behind. There was no protection; they were illuminated as if it were day.

"Fasten your seat belt," Glenn said quietly.

She fumbled with the catch, all fingers and thumbs, and the car behind overtook and swung itself into them with a thud that should have sent them crashing into the barrier.

Glenn smiled and changed into third gear. He had no difficulty in maintaining control. "Hang on," he said softly as the other car prepared for another swing.

The tyres tore across the road, the frame rocked and rattled, but Glenn kept on going with Melody hanging on for grim death, her teeth gritted tightly together.

They were neck and neck along the narrow road with Glenn starting to pull away when he said softly, "I'm going to stop dead before their next swing," and almost before he'd finished speaking he was standing on the brakes and the other car was swinging in on empty space, turning around, the back tyres scrambling over the edge of the road and then slowly, and then with increasing momentum, going backwards down the hillside.

Glenn had shot away the moment the road was clear but he stopped as they started to roll and got out to stand on the edge of the road.

Melody glanced quickly at his face. He was no longer smiling but there was no regret or horror on his face. He watched impassively as a tongue of flame reached up to the sky and then the car exploded, debris and flame and gigantic red sparks flying out in all directions.

He turned and got back into the car without making any comment.

"Hadn't we better do something?" Melody said uncertainly as he set the car in motion again.

"We'll tell the police. There's nothing we can do for them."

"But supposing they were flung clear? They could be lying out there injured . . . And in this cold . . ."

He regarded her curiously. "They were trying to kill us. Did you realise that?"

"No!"

"If they'd wanted to stop us they could have cut across and blocked the road right at the beginning."

"They panicked easily. They probably weren't thinking straight."

He shrugged. "Well, they'll do no more thinking."

"How can you be so cool about it?" she demanded hotly. "And when they were bumping us you were smiling. I saw you."

"You mean my teeth were bared?" He grinned. "Desperation, Melody. The fixed mask of grim terror."

She opened her mouth. Closed it again. He'd deny it. But he'd enjoyed those minutes when she'd been paralysed with fear. She was as strung up and tense as a taut violin string her fingers still twined between the leather strap-hold on the door, and he was as pleasantly relaxed as if he'd done nothing more stimulating than take an afternoon stroll.

148

She put her hands in her lap and tried to convince herself that most men enjoyed danger, that Glenn was not abnormal because of his superb skill at the wheel and his lack of emotion at being the cause of death of two men. Their lives or the lives of Eddy and Les? Was that what he had thought? Couldn't he have pulled away with the superior speed of his engine?

She couldn't ask him. She felt nervous; half afraid of him; half appalled at his callous disregard for death. She couldn't stop thinking of that explosion and the fiery furnace that had resulted and she wanted to be home with her family, where every action was predictable, where nothing was strange.

It was almost nine o'clock before they turned into the avenue. A car was parked outside her aunt's house but it drew away before they were near enough to see who was in it.

Glenn helped her out of the car. Her muscles were stiffening up and she was aching in every limb.

Her aunt and father were in the living room. Her father was in his chair, his head in his hands and her aunt was stooped over him, trying to comfort him.

"Hello," Melody said shakily as neither looked up.

Aunt Prudence froze as her father stared in disbelief, and then a discordant moan bubbled out of her lips and she keeled over in a dead faint.

"Melody!" Her father sprang heedlessly over the unconscious form of his sister and rushed over to her, touching her face, her arms, her shoulders, as if to assure himself he wasn't dreaming. "Melody!"

She buried her face against her father's chest. She wanted to cry. Silly now. When it was all over. "I've had a rotten time," she gulped.

"Come and sit down." Her father led her to the couch where Glenn had lifted Aunt Prudence. It was only then that he noticed what had happened to her.

"She's coming round," Glenn said as

her eyes flew open and she moaned like a wild banshee.

"It's all right," Glenn told her, comprehending where Melody merely stared. "It really is Melody, not someone playing a horrible trick. She's been rolling about in some coal but she's quite safe."

Her aunt's eyes swivelled over to Melody and she burst into tears. Aunt Prudence, who prided herself on her brisk unsentimentality!

Melody sat down beside her.

"He said you were in his hands," her aunt said chokingly. "He said we'd get a letter first, and then a finger every day until he had the jewels."

"It doesn't matter. Forget all about it. I'm here, I got away."

"Forgive me, forgive me." Her aunt struggled up to her feet and blundered out of the room.

"What happened?" her father asked quietly.

Glenn told him in a few brief sentences and her father nodded. The grey look was back on his face. "We called the police as

151

soon as we got that phone call. They've only just gone. They said they couldn't help, that I'd better do as the man demanded and hand over the jewels."

"They wouldn't do anything?" Glenn said incredulously.

"Oh, they wrapped it up," her father said wearily. "But that's what it amounted to. In their eyes I'm a criminal. I asked for this to happen once I stepped outside the law. They said they'd be round tomorrow to see the letter and arrange for any further calls to be taped."

"I'll go round and see them straight away," Glenn said. "What was the name of the senior officer?"

"I'm sorry. I wasn't taking in names." Her father leaned back in his chair, pressing the tips of his fingers over his forehead. "Phone them from here. No need for you to go to them."

"I'll have to sign a statement. Two men are dead."

"Men!" her father ejaculated. "Scum! To take a young girl and threaten her so cruelly. How much more have we to suffer? I thought the nightmare was over."

"It won't be over until the jewels turn up," Glenn said, carefully looking at neither of them.

Melody stiffened. Her father straightened up. He regarded Glenn with a dignity that made Melody's heart turn over. "I don't know where they are," he said in a low, firm voice. "And that's the truth."

Glenn held his gaze and then he nodded. There was an expression that Melody took for regret on his face. "I'll be seeing you," he said.

Neither Melody nor her father made a move to see him out of the house.

"He didn't believe me," her father said dully. "No one believes me."

"Don't be silly. He didn't say he didn't believe you." Melody ran over to her father but she knew it was true. Glenn had his doubts even if he did like her father.

Her father held her for a moment and then pushed her back, trying to smile at her. "You'd better have a bath before you give anyone else the fright you gave your aunt. Have you seen yourself?"

"No, but I can imagine it." She kissed him on the cheek and went wearily up the stairs. Every step seemed to take more energy than she possessed.

She looked in the mirror and couldn't believe what she saw. Staring eyes in a face that might have been hewn from the bowels of the earth. Even her hair was black.

She took off her clothes and sank into the bath. Aunt Prudence had run the water and put in half a bottle of her favourite bath essence. Apart from her reddened eyes she was herself again, with perhaps a slightly increased astringency to make up for her display of emotion.

Melody murmured yes and no in the right places, not really listening. It was enough to be able to relax under such comforting normality. She made no protest when she was bundled straight off to bed as soon as her hair was dry. She'd had some soup. She was warm and clean again. She slept like a log but dreamed of the rats and woke up moaning with terror.

"It's all right, Melody." Michael's voice was oddly adult. "Go back to sleep."

She sat up in bed, switching on the lamp. He was in his dressing gown in the armchair.

"What do you think you're doing here?" she demanded in astonishment.

"Keeping watch. Shut up."

He'd been strangely subdued the night before. Banished to his room when the police arrived and missing all the excitement of her return, he felt cheated and unimportant.

Melody looked at him and understood. "I must admit I would feel safer with you here," she said softly and was rewarded by the unconscious straightening of his shoulders and a look of pride and gratification on his face. He said casually, "I thought you would. Don't you worry, Melody. No one is going to get hold of you again. Not while I'm around."

She smiled and put the light out, settling down once more. In a little while she heard the tenor of his breathing change and she got up stealthily and draped her eiderdown over him.

She didn't dream again and when she woke up the eiderdown was back on her bed and there was no sign of Michael, only her aunt with a breakfast tray.

"You're not going in to work today," she announced with a martial light in her eyes as if expecting argument, but Melody only nodded.

She didn't want to go in, she didn't want to face Glenn, and she had no inclination to battle with that awful typewriter. There wasn't a square inch of her body that didn't ache or hurt in one way or another.

Alarmed at such lethargy her aunt announced that she'd better stay in bed and Melody didn't argue about that either.

"Has father gone to work?"

"Yes, he's gone." Her aunt glanced at the clock. "And I must fly. I'll come back at lunchtime and cook you something. Don't answer the door to anyone."

"All right." Melody picked at her breakfast and put the tray down on the floor with the food hardly touched. She thought she might read but it seemed too much trouble to go downstairs for a book. It was pleasant to lie in bed and do nothing at all. She drifted into a semi-doze but all at once she was wide awake, her body tense.

Someone was coming up the stairs.

She knew it was silly to stay where she was, that she should be hiding or looking for some kind of weapon with which to defend herself, but she could only stare at the door with the intense mesmerised stare of a trapped rabbit.

The sight of Michael was such an anti-climax she almost fell out of bed.

"What's the matter with you?" he demanded in alarm.

"Nothing." Not for the world would she admit how frightened she'd been. "Why aren't you at school?"

"I thought I'd better get back," he said with off-handed nonchalance."

"And what do you think can happen? In daytime, neighbours all around, bolts and locks on the doors, a phone in the house, every window closed! Father and Aunt Prudence wouldn't have left me if they'd thought there was any danger."

"Father phoned the police again. He told them he wanted someone to keep an eye on the house. *He* thinks they might try again."

Michael went over to the window and studied the area outside like a general sizing up a hostile piece of enemy territory.

"No, he doesn't. He's being careful, that's all. Besides those men are dead."

"I know. Father told me all about it and said I had to be very careful. Stay in the crowd, don't talk to any strange men. Honestly! He thinks I'm still a baby."

Oh dear. That had rankled. Rocking their still precarious relationship.

Melody said gently. "He's afraid for

you. Don't blame him for being over protective."

"Yes, yes. I understand." Michael turned away from the window. "I'll check the front of the house. Do you want anything?"

"No, thanks. Aunt Prudence is coming back at lunchtime. You'll cop it if she finds you here."

Michael grinned. "Thanks for the warning. I'll make sure she doesn't."

He went off whistling but a second later came rushing back to her room. "There's a car at the gate with two men in it."

The bell rang. Michael gulped. "What shall we do?"

They stared at one another. The bell rang again and then there was a loud hammering on the door.

Melody got out of bed and reached for her robe. "We'll see who it is. You stand by the phone."

He followed her downstairs "Put the chain on."

"Yes." Never mind the chain. She wasn't even going to open the door. She lifted the flap of the letter box gingerly, standing well back so that they couldn't poke anything at her. "Who is it?"

"Police." The voice was curt and hard with authority.

"Ask for their identification," Michael hissed.

"Yes." She said breathlessly, "Could I see your identification, please?"

It was held through the letter box and she snatched it away from the protruding finger and thumb, examining it intently. It seemed genuine. Det.-Sgt. Bolton. She opened the door within the confines of the chain.

"We'll just check with the police station that you're who you say you are," she said.

"That's all right, Miss Ford." He sounded resigned more than annoyed at the delay and leaned against the wall. "Green Street Police Station."

He was cadaver thin, with a huge beak of a nose and a mouth that was twisted in a permanent downward expression. The man with him was of medium height with a hard cynical face and eyes that looked as if they'd never sparkled in his life.

Melody regarded that one doubtfully and went back to Michael. "Don't policemen have to be over a certain height?" she whispered.

"Not now." He was a mine of information. "They had to relax the regulations because of the shortage of men."

"Oh! He said they were from Green Street Station. They don't seem worried that we're checking up on them."

"Never mind. It could be a bluff. They might think we won't phone if they're confident enough."

Michael phoned directory enquiries and asked for the number of the station and then he dialled. He sounded calm and collected. Melody listened in awe. This last couple of days she was learning things about her brother.

"You can let them in," he said, putting the receiver down.

She took the chain off and opened the door. Michael stepped forward. "I think this is yours, sir." He handed over the identity card. "I presume you've come to see my sister so I'll make some coffee. Would you care for some?"

Bolton regarded him in surprise and some amusement. "Well, thanks. It's very kind of you."

Melody restrained an impulse to giggle. Michael was determined he wasn't going to be banished this time.

She asked the two men to sit down and Bolton promptly took her father's chair. The other man preferred to wander around the room.

"You know why we're here," Bolton said. "We have Mr. Hunter's statement but we would also like to have one from you."

"Were the two men killed?"

"Oh yes." He sounded as callously indifferent as Glenn. "Now tell me what happened. Right from the beginning."

Michael came in with the coffee when she was describing the cellar. He'd used the instant coffee in the big breakfast mugs and as she mentioned the rats the tray swayed in his hand and he stood

162

stock still his eyes as round as gooseberries. "I bet you screamed blue murder. You're scared stiff of—"

"Thank you for the coffee, Michael," Melody put in pointedly.

"Oh sure, yes." He handed it round and then stood in the doorway, fixing his eyes suspiciously on the man wandering around.

"Are you going to guard her?" he demanded when Melody came to the end of her story.

Bolton's twisted mouth jerked upwards in a meaningless smile. "And you? And your aunt? And your father? We haven't the men and it's pointless anyway. We couldn't watch for ever. If anyone else is after you all they have to do is wait."

"That's not very comforting, is it?" Michael said, deep disapproval written all over his face.

"No, but that's how it is." He shrugged and turned to Melody. "When you're feeling better come down to the station and sign a statement. There's no hurry."

"They don't care at all," Michael said in disgust as Melody shut the door behind them.

"They're right though. How many men would it take to protect us all?" She sat down. Her coffee had gone cold.

"I don't like that one that never said a word. Prowling around as if he expected to spot the flipping jewels hidden here."

"I suppose you can't blame them. It's their job to be suspicious." She was suddenly weary. "I'm going back to bed."

"You do that. And don't worry about a thing." He patted her shoulder awkwardly. "I'll organise something."

She had a lump in her throat as big as a beach ball. "Thanks, Michael."

The police might not care what happened to her but Michael did. She could see him organising an army of schoolboys to protect her. Would Glenn be so concerned? She expected him to phone, or at least ask how she was after her ordeal, but the phone remained silent and when Aunt Prudence returned at

164

lunchtime she knew by the look on her face that she had bad news.

"Did you phone in?" she asked slowly.

Her aunt nodded reluctantly, "Brace yourself, Melody," she said. "You're not going to like this. Glenn has gone back to London."

6

"MAYBE it's best this way," her aunt said.

"I expect it is." She tried to put a brave face on it—no one was going to feel sorry for her—but inside she felt as though she were bleeding from an open wound.

It was very hard to smile and act normally when her father returned, his enthusiasm still waxing strong after his first day with Miles.

"He's not changed a thing," he said. "Even my father's desk is still there. And he's moved out of my room and gone back to his own old one. He couldn't have been nicer."

Melody listened and tried to make the right rejoinders. Her aunt and Michael were having no difficulty. Maybe there was something wrong with her. Maybe she was too hard on Miles. He could genuinely want her father back for no other reason than that put forward by her aunt.

She didn't feel like going in to work the next day but Aunt Prudence considered it would do her no good to be moping at home on her own. One day's invalidism was all she was allowed, despite all her multi-coloured bruises and the torn skin on her legs and hands.

She went to see Mr. Travis as soon as she'd taken her coat off but was told he'd be out for most of the day, so she collected the files and went on with her work. Maybe Glenn would be back. Maybe not. But the job would have to be finished.

Mr. Travis was in when she returned the files at the close of the day. He glanced up from a paper he was studying and said, "Drop them on the desk, Melody. I'll put them away."

"I was wondering . . . Is Gl—is Mr. Hunter returning?"

His face closed up. "Mr. Hunter is not answerable to me in any respect. I can't help you, Melody." Both expression and the tone of his voice forbade any further questions but she pressed on.

"On Friday, you were going to tell me something. What was it?"

"Friday? Friday?" he mused and tried for a paternal smile which failed miserably. His eyes didn't match. They were strained and anxious. "A lot has happened since Friday. I can't remember every little thing."

He was lying and she knew it. His eyes went down and he picked up his pen and started writing.

She stared at him in bewilderment. "I don't understand. Why should you be scared of him? You were going to warn me. What about? Tell me, Mr. Travis, please."

"Scared? I'm not scared." He bristled and straightened up in his chair but was still unable to meet her eyes for more than a second.

"If you say so," she said sadly. She wasn't going to get anything out of him. Not now. Whatever his intention on

Friday, something had happened to make him change his mind.

She turned for the door. "Goodnight, Mr. Travis."

He didn't answer and she glanced over her shoulder.

He was staring blankly ahead of him.

She hesitated and then closed the door gently behind her.

The girl in the outer office was covering up the typewriter. "Five o'clock," she said cheerfully. "Isn't it the most beautiful time of the day?"

Melody nodded absently. "It can't come fast enough. Did Mr. Hunter see Mr. Travis before he left?"

"*Did* he!" the girl said feelingly. "First thing Monday morning—and Mr. Travis like a cat on hot bricks ever since! I'll say he saw him."

"Do you know what they were talking about?" She had a peculiar sensation in the pit of her stomach. She could trust him, he'd said. But could she?

The girl applied her lipstick with a

lavish hand. "Not a clue. They shut up like clams when I went into the office."

"Did he mention when he would be back?"

"You're dashing Mr. Hunter wouldn't confide in me." She picked up her bag and was gone before Melody could pose another question.

It was raining when she got outside. She put up her umbrella and trudged along the pavement, too dispirited to dodge the bulldozing umbrella users, but when a car slid alongside and the door opened in front of her she sheered away like a fleet-footed gazelle and had gone two hundred yards before she recognised Natalie's plaintive cry. "Melody, Melody! It's only me."

She stopped, feeling all sorts of a fool. The Rolls caught up with her again and slid to a halt beside her. Natalie's vivid face was peering at her in concern. "Get in, child. Out of this dreadful rain. Why did you run away like that?"

Melody sank back against the luxurious upholstery, dropping her umbrella at her

170

feet and feeling guilty at the enormous amount of rain she seemed to have brought in with her.

"I suppose I'm nervous. You've not seen father since Sunday?"

"No." There was a question in Natalie's denial and her expression sharpened. "Something's happened, hasn't it? To you?"

"I was kidnapped."

The bald statement made Natalie pale. "What happened?" she whispered.

"It was on the way home on Sunday . . ." Melody told her tale once more. She was getting word perfect but still couldn't control her voice when she described the exploding car.

"They were killed," Natalie repeated. Her colour still hadn't returned. "But you think they were working for someone else?"

Melody nodded.

"Well, I don't know what your father is thinking of," Natalie exploded. "Why couldn't he tell me about it? Not a word!

171

And what is he doing about it? It could happen again."

"He's asked the police for help but they seem to think it would be a waste of time. No one would try anything while they were watching but as soon as they were pulled off it would be open season again. I can't be taken care of for ever—and there's Michael too. And Aunt Prudence. The detective pointed all that out."

"Well, I'm going to do something about it if no one else will," Natalie said determinedly. "I'll have to think about it." She leaned forward. "You're coming to dinner with me. We'll phone your father from the flat."

Melody began to feel better. She enjoyed being with Natalie. Her father was right when he said she was like a breath of fresh air.

The flat was on the second floor of a pleasant colonial-type building with white stuccoed walls, painted shutters, vines and creepers trailing artistically around the windows. It was furnished in more modern style than her home in the country but there was the same superb taste and comfort.

"Phone your father right away," Natalie said. "We don't want him worrying. I'll see how things are in the kitchen." She vanished through a door at the end of the wide sitting room.

Melody phoned home. Michael answered and she told him to apologise to Aunt Prudence and explain she was having dinner with Natalie.

"I didn't mess up any plans for this evening, did I?" Natalie asked, emerging from the kitchen with a huge white apron wrapped around her curvaceous hips. "I'm not usually so dictatorial but you rather took the wind out of my sails."

"No plans. Only Aunt Prudence cooking my dinner. She won't mind."

"No handsome Mr. Hunter?"

"I've not seen him since Sunday," Melody said shortly. "Or heard from him."

Natalie's eyebrows went up and she pursed her mouth quizzically, but wisely refrained from comment.

They were having coffee before she told Melody why she had been waiting for her. "I meant to pick you up outside work," she said. "But I had a last minute phone call. Everything is arranged."

There was a pleased smile on her face. "I had a meeting with Robert Gant first thing on Monday. Ex-Yard man, highly recommended; discreet, efficient and with the biggest organisation in town. They've got a girl starting tomorrow. She'll take the place of Miles's secretary. They fixed the camera in position last night and on Friday I've arranged for Meg Cameron, a friend of mine, to take her jewellery in to be cleaned." Her smile was beatific. "What do you think of that?"

"I feel a little scared," Melody admitted slowly. "You're breaking the law for my father."

"Phooey!" Natalie dismissed that airily.

"How did you manage to get the secretary to leave?"

"Well, I suggested they offer her a couple of hundred pounds and a free holiday in Europe if she took off without a word. I don't know if they did that and I'm not going to ask. I don't really want to know the whys and wherefores. The end justifies the means—in this case at least. And I had quite enough on my plate persuading Meg to take her jewels out of the bank. She treats them as an investment, not a pleasure. Silly woman."

"Did you tell her why?"

"Lord no! She would never have agreed if she thought we were asking for them to be stolen. I told her I wanted to do your father a favour and put him in well with Miles by bringing people to the shop again."

"Supposing something goes wrong?"

"We won't think of that," Natalie said emphatically. "It's a very simple plan. Simple plans succeed. I'm adding my necklace for good measure. Remember it?" She pushed her chair back and went over to the small wall safe concealed beneath a picture.

The diamonds Melody had last seen around her own neck glittered in Natalie's hand, emitting the cold pure flashes of liquid light that had held her spellbound.

"I've broken the clasp on it," Natalie said. "And I'll take it in on Friday morning too. Meg is not going to mention my name, of course. It will be a coincidence too good for a thief to pass by."

Melody stared at the stones and a cold premonition trickled over her spine.

It was too beautiful, too irresistible. Her father would see it again. Supposing he succumbed to temptation as he did before. Their careful trap might catch the man they were trying to protect.

She looked at Natalie. She was gazing at the diamonds thoughtfully and then she glanced up and met Melody's eyes and Melody knew the same thought had occurred to her. "You won't breathe a word of this to your father, will you?"

She shook her head, too choked up to speak. Natalie had doubts then. She was going to find out the truth whatever it cost her. She had courage and loyalty but she had to know for certain. Melody couldn't blame her. Blind faith didn't come easily. She wanted desperately to warn her father but she knew such a betrayal of Natalie's trust was a betrayal of her father himself. If she couldn't believe in him she might as well point a gun at his head herself. There would be nothing left between them.

Natalie returned the diamonds to the safe and refilled their coffee cups. "A liqueur?" she asked. "Or brandy?"

"No, nothing thanks."

"You don't mind if I do?" She poured herself an outsize brandy, swirling it around in the balloon glass. "And until Saturday," she added, "I think you should be out of circulation, where no one can touch you. And Michael too. What would you say to staying at the cottage?"

"I can't. There's my job."

"Do you enjoy it, Melody?"

"Well, it's a living."

"A very dull one it seems to me." She regarded Melody speculatively over the rim of her glass. "I could get you a far more interesting one. I know a lot of people. Think about it and I'll make some enquiries. Would you like to travel for instance?"

"I think I would," Melody said slowly. "I like seeing new places." And new faces too. Give up her job? Why not? Especially if Mr. Travis didn't want her back.

"Have you any French or German?"

"We did them at school but I couldn't say I was fluent at either."

"We could soon put that right if you have the groundings." She lit a cigarette. "But that's for the future. I think you should go down to the cottage tomorrow. Explain at work. I'm sure they'll understand."

"They don't know about my father."

"Oh, my dear." Natalie looked disconcerted. "Don't you think that a mistake? It's never wise to hide things like that. They find out one way or another and then it looks bad because you've tried to keep it quiet."

"Well, they might know now. Glenn could have told Mr. Travis. He's been acting very strangely with me."

"You think Glenn would do that?"

"I don't know." She stared listlessly at the table with its Swedish dinnerware and cutlery. "He's not been in to work since Monday morning and he's not phoned or anything. London's not the other end of the world. He could have called to see how I was—unless he had a guilty conscience and couldn't bring himself to speak to me."

"You're in love with him, aren't you?" Natalie said gently.

"I don't know." She turned her cup around restlessly. "I thought I was but I don't know him. How can you love someone when you don't know what kind of a person they are?"

"It's easy," Natalie said dryly. "The problem is usually remaining in love when you know exactly what they are. Don't worry about him. I think he'll be back."

"How can you say that? You don't know him either."

"Maybe not. But I've seen men like him before. They play the field, no one ever thinks they'll marry and then

179

suddenly all at once it happens. I don't suppose he's met anyone like you before and I'm quite sure he won't be able to forget you."

Melody gave an unwilling smile. "You're better than Aunt Prudence at trying to cheer me up."

"You'll see." Natalie finished her brandy. "I think I'll come home with you and talk to your father about hiding low for a while. I think I can persuade him without saying it shouldn't be for very long."

She rang for her chauffeur and told him to be outside in twenty minutes.

"Does he live here too?" Melody asked curiously.

"Oh yes. Next door as a matter of fact. I like him to be on hand. I'm a target. You'll have realised that of course. A wealthy woman living on her own! But I take precautions. This flat is more vulnerable than the cottage but I've only to touch a button on my desk and its emergency stations for Tom. There's a special lock on the door and the windows are wired. Come to think of it, if you don't fancy the idea of leaving your job you could stay here for the next few days. And Michael too—if you don't mind sharing a room." She warmed to the idea. "Why didn't I think of it before? It would be rather nice to have you both."

"We couldn't. It's too much for you."

"Nonsense. The perfect solution. Your father couldn't argue about that. Come along. I'll talk to him."

But her father was extremely reluctant to agree to it. "It's not your problem, Natalie," he said stiffly. "And I don't think anything could happen here in the town. Michael and Melody are sensible people. They're not going to be taken in by any more crooks who want to get them on their own. So they stay with you? For how long? You've got your own life to lead and so have the children. I don't want them to lead an abnormal life from now on."

"You're an idiot, Peter. Your stupid pride again. You think any kind of help is charity. Consider it sensibly. Melody believes those two men were working for someone. The earliest that someone could find out that something has gone wrong with his plan would be yesterday. Give him another twenty-four hours for him to find out what and start working out another way to get at you and then you're in trouble again."

She started pacing the floor. Melody watched in admiration. She didn't even pause for thought.

"Is that what you want? Even if I have Michael and Melody for only a few days, it's a few days of complete safety and during that time anything could happen. This man, whoever he is, could be picked up by the police. He could be run over by a bus." The things that could happen tripped easily off her tongue.

"Don't you see," she continued. "We've got nothing to lose by being careful. The longer we keep it up the better."

Her father sighed heavily. "What do you think, Melody? Does all that sound logical to you?"

Inventive, hardly logical. She said gently, "It could happen like that. Let us go, father, and you'll have an easier mind."

"Will I be driven to school in the Rolls?" Michael demanded in awe.

"My goodness me, there'll be no holding you," Aunt Prudence said caustically. "Give them your blessing, Peter. Let him have his moments of glory."

"It's not as if you won't be seeing them," Natalie said. "I'll expect you both to dinner every night and at the week-end we'll go to the cottage."

Melody and Michael left them discussing the details and went upstairs to pack some clothes and then Natalie bore them off and installed them in her spare bedroom, a large comfortable room with twin beds and plenty of storage space.

Melody unpacked while Michael made a tour of the flat, finding out all about the security system and how it worked.

It was quite late when they went to bed but Natalie had them up early and their breakfast on the table.

Melody protested. She had a good idea Natalie didn't normally get up until much later.

"I don't want to hear another word about it," Natalie said. "I'm going to enjoy looking after you. I never had any children—not that we planned it that way. When we got married we had decided on six children." For a moment her eyes were wistful but then she smiled and shrugged. "But no one can have everything they want in this world. Now I think Tom had better drop you first, Melody, and then take Michael on to school. Do you agree?"

"Yes, Michael starts at nine, later than me."

"And you finish at five. Tom will be waiting right outside for you. He'll have had plenty of time to pick Michael up and bring him back here. Now let me see . . . what about your aunt and father . . ."

Melody left her arranging Tom's time-table quite happily, fitting in her shopping, a lunch date, a hair appointment.

It was raining again. She sat in luxury

in the back of the car with Michael reflecting how nice it was not to be standing at the bus stop getting wet and rattling about in a crowded bus.

Michael must have been thinking along the same lines. He said enviously, "It's great to be rich, isn't it?"

"It helps. See you tonight." She was out of the car, running across the pavement to the giant insurance building before Tom had time to get out of the car and help her out with the ceremony he bestowed on Natalie.

He gave her a wave as she glanced back from under the sheltering portals and Michael wound down his window and called cheekily, "Remember now! Don't go talking to any strange men."

She was smiling as she went inside but it died away as she got into the lift and the depression hit her again.

Natalie had the right idea. She would get a new job, a more interesting one, one that wouldn't give her any time to think about herself—or anyone else. She would write her notice out right away.

She took her coat off and started on a rough draft in long hand. She'd type it out when she'd decided what to say. The simple way was best, no explanations. If Mr. Travis wanted to know why she wanted to leave he could always ask.

She lifted the cover off her typewriter and saw there was a sheet of paper caught in the roller. A note from Mr. Travis asking her to look up the file of a past employee.

Her mouth turned down. All the old records were kept in the basement, a gloomy, dusty cavern piled high to the roof with stacks of files from the year dot.

She went straight down. It didn't occur to her that there was anything strange in the request. The temporary secretary wouldn't have had a clue where to look.

The personnel files were over at the far side. Each department had their own row theoretically but Mr. Travis's section spilled over onto other departments' allocations wherever there was room and she was on her knees searching in vain for the name Mr. Travis had given her when the light went out.

She swore under her breath. It wasn't completely dark. There were gratings in the pavement above and the door to the side entrance which went up onto a narrow street at the back of the building had a top of frosted glass.

It was enough to see where she was going but she couldn't read the names on the files. She made her way to the stairs carefully. She'd have to get one of the maintenance men to put in a new bulb and he'd grumble at her as if it was her fault it needed replacing.

A small sound distracted her attention. She paused, her foot on the bottom stair. Mice? It was possible in all these stacks of paper. And then without any further warning something was slapped across her mouth.

She struggled instinctively, her breath drawn in for the scream that was gagged back by the stuff over her mouth.

A sack was dragged over her head and

right down over her body and she was swung up and over someone's shoulder.

She panicked completely then, disoriented, blinded and dumb, her kicks hampered by the sack and the arms holding her tight. There was no room to move, no room to breathe, her throat bubbled with sound that roared in her ears but was muffled to anyone who might hear. She was being carried away like a sack of old rubbish. And dumped like it too.

She forced herself to lie still, fighting the fear that stopped her thinking. She had been carried out by the basement exit to the side street. She was in a vehicle of some sort. She heard the slam of the door and then the engine started up and they were moving.

She couldn't believe it. She had been kidnapped again. After all those precautions. How had they known she'd be in the basement? The note! Mr. Travis! Did this explain his odd behaviour? Was he being forced to help these men who thought they could make her father hand over the jewels in return for her safety? Had he perhaps been going to warn her about that first attempt on Friday night and not about Glenn as she had supposed? But no . . . He'd mentioned Glenn specifically. The note had been typed. It was probably not from Mr. Travis at all. But it had to be someone who knew the system.

Her mind whirled. Something rolled onto her feet making her realise they were free. She managed to sit up. The sack was not secured in any way. She pulled it off and cautiously groped around her in the dark. She was in a van of some sort. Her hand went to her mouth. It was sticking plaster there—a great expanse of it. Whoever had slapped it across her mouth had made plenty of allowances for not hitting it square on.

She pulled it off gingerly, a bit at a time. Not for her the quick skin pulling rip off. There was no one to see what a coward she was.

It was a can of Coke that had rolled on her feet. She pulled the ring off and lifted it to her mouth. The liquid fizzed up and ran over her mouth and down her neck, but she was thirsty. The shock had made her throat as dry as tinder. She held the empty can of Coke in her hand. They'd have to stop for a traffic light and when they did she'd make such a noise someone would have to investigate.

She tried experimentally banging against the side of the van and got a shock. There was almost no noise at all. A layer of rubber covered the surface completely.

She crawled to the end of the van but there was no inner handle. She wasn't going to find an escape hatch from this prison.

Her groping hands came up against a cardboard carton, half full. She could feel a couple more cans of coke, sandwiches, an apple and an orange.

A thoughtful captor.

The speed increased. She guessed they were on a motorway.

Further exploration revealed her coat and handbag. She went for the torch at once but discovered nothing she hadn't found out already.

A small van lined with thick black rubber. She switched the torch off again to conserve the battery. It never lasted for very long and there was no knowing what lay at the end of this journey.

She checked the time at intervals and at midday ate the sandwiches and had another Coke.

It was impossible to tell where she was being taken. There was little to be heard above the noise of the engine, but soon after she'd eaten she guessed they were off the motorway. Their steady speed was curtailed and then after about another hour they were twisting and turning around corners and going up and down hill.

She was halfway through the apple when the van slowed and came to a standstill. She picked up the full can of Coke. It was the best weapon to hand. Standing poised at the end of the van, she tensed for the moment when the doors were opened and she could leap down on her kidnapper.

The jerking wrench of the van nearly knocked her off balance but it travelled for only a few yards and then came to a standstill again and this time the engine was cut.

She heard the key turn, the handle pulled down and then the doors were pulled forward fractionally. And then there was silence.

She waited until the tension became unbearable and then pushed forward a tentative finger. Were they waiting for her to make the first move? Realising the danger of opening the doors themselves?

The van doors fell back at her touch. It was dark outside. A garage, she guessed.

She crashed both doors back and jumped down, holding the torch before her, spinning round frantically to pinpoint the enemy but she never saw a thing. She only felt the grip around her arms and then something sweet and overpowering was in her nostrils. Chloroform. She tried to jerk her head away but a cloth reeking of the stuff was put over her

192

nose and mouth and her struggles weakened until they stopped completely.

She awoke to a room bathed in a pink light from a small bedside lamp. For a moment she lay blinking at the ceiling, and then she turned on her side. It was a small room with a low ceiling, the walls were papered in a smooth white and the floorboards stained and polished to a glossy black. There was no window and the door was of thick oak. It looked old and immovable.

She sat up and pulled back the electric blanket which covered her. There were no sheets and the mattress was encased in a stoutly sewn piece of denim. She was wearing a silky transparent nightdress that fell to her feet as she stood up.

A note was propped up against the lamp. Block capitals, uncompromising and abrupt, and not at all reassuring despite the message.

"Do not worry about anything. You will

not be harmed if you behave yourself."

She stared at it in dismay and then her eyes fell on the boxes of food piled on the floor against the wall. There were packets of curry and spaghetti and other meals in the instant food range, enough tinned stuff to last her for a month, blocks of chocolate, tea and coffee, powdered milk, sugar, some fresh fruit and more of the cans of Coke.

A small electric stove was balanced on an orange box which contained a frying pan and a couple of saucepans, there was a pile of paper backs, a little transistor radio. Everything for her comfort. Not at all like the cellar.

She tried the door and was surprised when the latch lifted and it opened easily but then realised she shouldn't have been with all this attention to detail. It opened into a bathroom and the door from that was securely locked. She peered through the big, old fashioned keyhole but the key was missing.

She was in some kind of cottage from

the look of the doors and the low ceilings. There was a tiny window of frosted glass high up on the wall, the wall itself about three feet in thickness. She balanced on the lavatory seat, doubting whether she could squeeze through the window but it was screwed down and she didn't fancy trying to break that glass.

A fresh toothbrush, still sealed in its Cellophane was propped in a glass, there was toothpaste too and two tablets of soap. Roger and Gallet. No expense spared. There was some of their bath salts too but the towel was threadbare and full of holes.

She looked down at her transparent nightdress and understood. Modesty was supposed to keep her from attempting to escape.

The cover sewn so firmly over the mattress. Probably impossible to remove. She's noticed the tin opener was one of the gadget type, useless for anything but the job it was designed for. She'd have laid a bet there was no knife provided, and she was right. There were two spoons, that was all, a small and a large one.

She stared thoughtfully at the electric blanket. It must have hurt him to provide that but did he bank on her being unwilling to risk freezing to death by messing about with it?

However, there was no point in worrying about clothing until she'd found a way out and she had until Friday. Her father had to be his normal self then, unharassed by an anxiety that might make him do something stupid. He might think it worth the risk to get any jewels in order to make an exchange for her freedom.

She made one of the curries and then tea.

He'd thought of everything; no clothes, no tools she could use, no furniture other than the bed and the small table on which the lamp rested.

She glanced through the paperbacks. They were all brand new; thrillers, romances, Penguin novels. She picked up one of the thrillers hoping it might give her some ideas but before she'd read many pages she felt her eyelids drooping.

She turned off the light. Time enough to make her escape in the morning. But during the night she was wakened abruptly by the light of a torch on her face.

Someone was in the room with her, someone watching her as she slept.

7

HER hand went straight to the bedside lamp but it failed to come on. She pressed the switch frantically and heard a soft laugh. "It's off at the mains."

She sat up sharply, shielding her eyes. "The last two men who tried to kidnap me died in agony," she cried. "You'd better let me go before something happens to you."

"And you'd better get back under the blanket," he advised her. "You're not decent."

The blanket was up to her throat before he'd finished speaking. She watched, hot with impotent anger as the beam danced around the room, checking once or twice before coming back to rest on her face. "Is there anything you need?" he asked.

"You seem to have thought of everything," she said bitterly, trying to see beyond the beam of the torch. He was just a shape in the darkness, a vague shadow. "When are you going to let me go?"

"Soon. Don't you be worrying." He had an accent. Irish? She couldn't decide. Of course it could be assumed. "I see you've recovered from the chloroform. I'm sorry I had to use that on you."

"I'm sure you are," she said heavily. "You're wasting your time keeping me here. My father didn't take those jewels."

He didn't answer. The beam just snapped off. She slid over to the other side of the bed as quickly and quietly as she could, suddenly afraid and apprehensive. She couldn't hear a sound. She listened intently and then could bear it no longer.

"Do you hear me?" she cried.

The bedside lamp suddenly flicked into light as if in answer and she jumped violently. But the room was empty. He had gone. She flung the blanket back and ran into the bathroom, tugging violently at the door. It was as securely locked as before.

He had moved as silently as a ghost. She came slowly back into the bedroom. There was a box at the foot of the bed. Bread, bacon, eggs and mushrooms, a pound of butter, a hunk of cheese.

She started to laugh hysterically. It was too much.

The sound of a car starting up silenced her. She listened to it dying away into the distance and soberly got back into bed. So he wasn't staying. He'd gone away again. For how long?

She shivered. The night air was cold. The blanket had lost its warmth. She curled up into a ball and tried to get back to sleep but it was hard. This attention to her comfort was all very well but what would he do when he didn't get what he wanted?

Sleep eluded her. When she thought it was morning she put the radio on. Another Irish voice announcing it was seven twenty-six. It was demoralising.

But she kept it on. It made her feel less alone.

She had a bath, made inroads into the provisions he'd brought for breakfast and then sat in the middle of the bed with the blanket draped around her determined to find a way out.

She'd slept, she'd had food, time to recover from the shock, time to think . . . and it was now time to move. No one could devise an escape proof prison.

Her gaze roamed the room. It was odd there was no window. Most rooms had windows, even old cottages like this one. Unless it had been bricked up when the window tax had been introduced. But it was in the big houses that one saw that scarred façade, and this couldn't be a big house. The whole feeling was wrong.

She got up. If she had more light . . . She took the pink shade off the lamp but the bulb was a low wattage and the removal of the shade increased the light hardly at all.

Going over to the walls she rapped her knuckles against as much of the area she could reach, feeling only the solid stone beneath the crusted anaglypta paper.

It was no use. And it was cold being away from the blanket.

She put some water on the stove to make coffee and while she was waiting for it to boil noticed what a long lead was on the stove. The plug was at the base of one of the other walls. It would surely have been more sensible to pile up all the stuff with the stove over there.

But he had a reason. He had a reason for everything he did.

She turned the stove off and dragged it away from the wall. And it was there. She could see it now. A square patch that was barely discernible. She ripped the wall-paper off with her finger nails. It was hardboard beneath, fitted into the square opening like a lid.

She ruined her nails and then had to admit defeat. She couldn't move it. If only she had a knife . . . something to slide in between.

She tried the spoon and felt a rush of triumphant pleasure when she managed to

202

force it through. He'd thought a spoon useless for anything but eating, had he? She'd show him.

She levered the hardboard away until she could get her hand over the edge and pull it away. It came with a rush and she blinked at the sudden daylight and could have cried in disappointment.

The size of the patch had made her think the window would be of fairly large proportions but it covered a narrowing embrasure which culminated in a tiny leaded window only inches larger than the one in the bathroom. She could never climb through it.

She couldn't even get it open, although it didn't appear to be screwed down.

She could smash it of course—with the pan. A quick, sharp thrust with the handle.

She averted her head, afraid of flying glass, and used both hands. The glass shivered and splintered. Her knuckles were bloodied as the handle went through and she caught the back of her hands against the pane.

So . . . one pane free. Where did that get her? She could shout through it. To whom?

There were fields ahead, a small wood, a line of hedgerows. No sign of a road. But there were cows in one of the fields. They had to be milked. Twice a day. Someone would come for them.

She brushed the glass away from the window seat. Someone had to pass sooner or later.

She had a quick sandwich for her lunch, keeping her eye on the window as she made it. When was milking time? Four o'clock? Five?

But before then she heard the sound of a car engine. One passing or coming to the cottage?

She listened intently. The car was sedately driven. She thought it was going past the cottage and then the engine died and there was silence again.

She flew into the bathroom with the frying pan in her hands. Stationing herself behind the door she waited tensely. The minutes passed. Maybe it wasn't the man returning. Maybe it was someone else just calling at the cottage. A postman . . . or someone trying to sell something. But she couldn't hear a bell ring and the car didn't start up again.

Her hopes started to dwindle. There was no reason for him to come up. Five minutes had passed. Then another ten.

And then without any warning sound the handle of the door turned, not slowly, more as if someone had expected just to walk in normally.

Melody held her breath and raised the pan high. But the door didn't open. Instead the handle went up an down again and a girl's voice called out cheerfully, "Glenn! Are you in there?"

Glenn! Melody stood frozen. The door was rattled, the handle jerking again, and there was a muttered sound of irritation and a bang on the door. "Glenn! Come on. I'm desperate."

Melody felt cold sweat on her forehead and yet she felt hot all over. She didn't know what do to. There was another muttered sound and then silence. The girl was going away.

Melody was galvanised into action. She banged on the door. "Hey! I'm locked in. Get me out, will you?"

There was a complete silence for several seconds. She wondered if the girl had heard her, but then she spoke. She sounded as if she was wondering if she'd been hearing things. "You're locked in?"

"Silly, isn't it?" Melody tried to make her voice light and easy with just a shade of embarrassment. "Is there a spare key anywhere?"

"But how—?" The girl cut herself short. "Hang on. I'll try the front door key. These old locks are often interchangeable."

She was away about five minutes and then Melody heard the scrape of a key in the lock. A moment later, the door swung forward and she was face to face with her rescuer, a strikingly attractive brunette in the chic grey uniform of an airline hostess. She possessed the sleek, poised sophistication that made air hostesses the world over stand out from the crowd, but the poise was not equal to an occasion such as this.

Her jaw dropped as her eyes went over Melody, going incredulously over the nightdress, drawn to the frying pan, back to Melody's face and then down to the pan again.

She swallowed visibly. "You're . . . er . . . a friend of Glenn's, I take it?"

"A very dear friend," Melody said expressionlessly. She stepped past the girl. She was on a tiny landing with two closed doors facing her. A flight of stairs led down into what was obviously the main room of the cottage.

It was long and fairly narrow, dominated by a huge stone fireplace. It was comfortably furnished; big chairs, warm colours, polished wood, a smooth fitted carpet and deep-rose drapes at the attractive long and elegant bay windows. There was no sign of her clothes.

The girl followed her down, seemingly unable to take her eyes from her. "It probably seems like an awfully silly question to you," she remarked diffidently. "But is there any significance to that frying pan you're clutching so fervently?"

"Oh! No." Melody stared at the frying pan vaguely. "Are you expecting to see Glenn this afternoon?"

"No. But then anything is possible with Glenn." Her eyes wandered over Melody again. "Anything!" she repeated. "May I ask who you are and what you're doing here?"

"My clothes must be somewhere," Melody said abruptly. "Have you any idea where they might have been put?"

"Your clothes!" The girl swallowed again. She said uncertainly. "I'll have a look for you."

She turned with obvious reluctance and went up the stairs again.

Melody went straight over to the couch where a handbag and grey cloak had been carelessly thrown over a zipped airline bag.

She opened the bag first; underclothes, a dress of fine silk, a pair of mules, makeup, a pack of cigarettes, perfume.

She could make do with that if her clothes were nowhere around.

She opened the handbag next, flipping through the contents, pulling out the passport, her ears cocked for the girl's return. Miss Katherine Dalton. The photograph didn't do her justice. Black hair, blue eyes, five foot seven inches. She was twenty-five years of age.

A drawer slammed shut. She pushed the passport back and was over by the fireplace when the girl came down the stairs. Her arms were full. She'd found the clothes and Melody's handbag was over her arm.

"Your clothes," she said in a peculiarly restrained voice.

"Thank you."

Melody took them from her and without any more ado pulled the nightdress over her head and started to dress.

The girl turned away. "I think I need a drink," she said in the same carefully restrained fashion. "Will you join me?"

"No, thank you. Is there a telephone here?"

"I'm afraid not."

"Where is this place?"

The girl had stopped pouring from the decanter she had picked up but at that she poured again and doubled her drink.

"You're in Walton-on-Stour," she said carefully, after taking a long swallow. "It's a little village in Surrey." She paused. "I looked in the back room. You weren't just locked in by accident, were you? It's stocked for a seige. How long have you been here?"

"Quite long enough," Melody said grimly. "Is today Thursday?"

"Yes."

Good. She'd been worried in case that chloroform had knocked her out for longer than she thought. She had plenty of time then. Her father would go in to work with his mind at rest tomorrow.

She pulled up the zip on her dress and stepped into her shoes. "Where is the nearest telephone?"

"In the village—about five miles away. I'll take you if you like."

"That's very kind of you."

210

"Oh, I have a condition. You must tell me what this is all about. What's Glenn up to now?"

"Glenn!" Melody didn't want to think about him. She couldn't believe he was responsible for keeping her here. She said slowly, "Glenn Hunter? Silver blond hair, brown eyes, tall and lean?"

"That's my Glenn."

Melody glanced surreptitiously at her left hand. No ring. But what did that mean these days? She had a key, she obviously knew her way around.

"How does kidnap and extortion strike you?" she said evenly.

"Kidnap and extortion!" The girl gave a peal of laughter. "You've got to be joking."

"I'm not. You said you've seen the room. I was locked in there. How much proof do you need?"

"But—No!" The girl stared at her in frank disbelief. "It's got to be some kind of joke. Extortion! What's Glenn supposed to want?"

"Some jewels he thinks my father is hiding."

"You've got it wrong. You have to be mistaken. Glenn's not like that."

"Well, I wouldn't know what he's like, but this cottage belongs to him, doesn't it?" She could hear him telling Aunt Prudence about it. The place where he could relax. Oh, Glenn . . .

"He owns it, yes," the girl admitted.

"And I don't suppose he was expecting you to arrive and mess things up for him."

The girl was slower in answering that. "I was scheduled for a three week trip," she said slowly. "I had to cancel. Even so . . . How is he supposed to have kidnapped you?"

"A sack over my head, a ride in a rubber-lined van, chloroform. I woke up here."

"A sack . . . ? And chloroform . . . ? To keep you from recognising him? So you don't know it's him really, do you?"

"It has to be."

"But he wouldn't have used this

212

cottage. That's stupid. And Glenn's not stupid. Far from it."

"He wasn't anticipating that I would find out, and maybe," she added bitterly, "he thought that if I did I wouldn't go to the police."

"Oh?" The girl carried her drink over to the couch and sat down, regarding Melody thoughtfully. "And was he right in that?"

"I think I will have that drink after all." Melody turned her back on the girl and headed for the tray. Yes. He was right. She wouldn't tell the police anything that would link his name with this kidnapping. She was still in love with him. "I suppose I would give him the benefit of the doubt," she said aloud. "It could have been anyone. He was careful. And when he came last night he'd turned the switch off at the mains. He thought of everything."

"He came last night?" the girl said in an odd voice.

"He only stayed a minute," Melody said quickly. "He brought some bread and bacon and stuff." She turned round, drink in hand, knowing what had immediately sprung to the girl's mind. "I don't imagine he'd ever have to make anyone captive for that," she said dryly.

A faint flush coloured the girl's cheeks, she looked uncomfortable and then surprisingly she uttered a soft laugh.

"It's ridiculous I know, but far more in character. Shades of the Sheik of Araby! Marry me or else! Now *that* I can picture Glenn doing. He's very high handed with his women."

"I am *not* one of his women."

The girl looked at her strangely. Had she been too emphatic? She said, "Well, then . . . If you're not going to the police what are you going to do?"

"Get back home as soon as possible."

"All right. I'll drive you to London. You can get an express from there and be home in no time at all."

As Melody stared, her eyelashes dipped and then rose again. "I'm afraid I looked in your bag," she said apologetically. "A shocking thing to do but the situation is most intriguing. You and Glenn . . . How long have you known him? And how did you meet?"

"I hardly know him at all. I was detailed to work for him while he completed an O and M survey at our branch, that was only a few days ago." But how long ago that seemed. So much had happened.

She was lost in thought for a moment and then became aware of the girl again. Her face had completely cleared of expression, almost as if she'd had a shock.

As Melody stared, she lowered her head, reaching for her bag, groping blindly and coming up with a cigarette case. She lit a cigarette but when she raised her eyes again there was nothing in her expression but the interest she had displayed before.

Melody went back over what she'd said. There'd been nothing of a startling nature there. Maybe she'd imagined that sense of shock. But the girl didn't ask any more questions. She said, "When you're ready, we'll leave."

Melody drained her glass and put on her coat. "I'd still like to make a phone call first," she said.

"As you wish."

She didn't bother locking the door of the cottage. Her car was a little Mini. There was a suitcase on the back seat. So she'd been planning on more than an overnight stay? Whether Glenn was there or not?

The lane in front of the cottage wandered between thick hedgerows to a sleepy looking village consisting of some dozen cottages and a general shop.

A black-browed woman of formidable proportions was ensconced behind the counter engaged in a comfortable conversation with two equally well endowed women who looked as if they had been there for the afternoon.

They broke off as the two girls entered, staring curiously. Melody tripped over a sack of potatoes; the floor was as hazardous as a mine field—crates of fruit and vegetables, stacks of tins, bottles of minerals and fruit squashes. But the girl was as sure-footed as a gazelle. She made her way to the counter, cheerfully greeting the woman. "How's things, Mrs. Bellaby? You're keeping well? The telephone is over there, Melody, in the corner. Shout out if you need any change. Hello, Mrs. Jones . . . Mrs. Carpenter."

Uncomfortably aware that the girl was not succeeding in attracting all the attention to herself Melody managed to make her way to the phone without falling over anything else. It was on a shelf, out in the open. They would hear every word she said.

The girl was being greeted in turn by the three women. They called her Kate and seemed to know her very well.

Melody picked up the receiver, hesitating before dialling the number home. The reaction had been bad enough last time when she'd only been missing a few hours and this time she couldn't give any details—not unless she wanted to set this village buzzing by the ears. Besides the phone could be tapped by the police. She couldn't let them trace where she was calling from.

She dialled Natalie's number instead.

The girl—Kate—was telling a story about being stranded in the Bahamas and missing out on a trip to somewhere else that sounded equally exotic.

Tom answered. She pressed the release button.

"Is Mrs. Galbreith there? It's Melody."

She heard the swift indrawn breath. "Are you all right, Miss?"

"Yes."

"We've been that worried . . . Hang on. I'll get her." There was a clunk in her ears and she heard him shouting.

"Mrs. Galbreith! Mrs. Galbreith! Come quickly. She's on the phone. She says she's all right."

Natalie pounced on the receiver, breathless and incoherent. "Melody! Is that really you? Are you *really* all right? Where are you? What happened?"

"I'm fine, I'm fine," Melody cut in hurriedly. "Will you pass the news on to my father? Tell him I'll be home some time later tonight. I'm going to London and I'll get a train from there. I don't know how long it will take."

"But Melody . . . Where are you? We've been nearly out of our minds with worry. They said you'd walked out at work. They showed me a letter of resignation you'd left on your desk. Were you forced to write that? Were you—Oh dear, Melody. I don't know what I'm saying. We've been waiting for a message. Your father's not left the phone for an instant. Nothing . . . no one phoning . . . The uncertainty's been driving us mad."

"Phone him now. Right away."

"Yes, yes. Melody—" The pips sounded, distracting with their stuttering signal.

Melody said hastily, "I'll have to go, I've no more change. I'll see you later. Don't worry."

She replaced the receiver and turned round.

Kate was still talking but from the expression on the women's faces they hadn't missed much of what was said on the phone either. Melody smiled at them. She didn't think she'd given them much to talk about.

"Thank God you said nothing about kidnapping and extortion there," Kate said fervently as they got back into the car. "For a horrible moment I thought I might have misjudged you."

"Misjudged me?"

"Well, you look the fairly sensible type. I could see their ears flapping and hoped you'd appreciate it. There I was talking the most awful drivel trying to catch what you said and drown you out at the same time. They thrive on gossip around here."

"So I'm the sensible type?" Melody said bitterly. "I'm glad you appreciate it."

"They wouldn't have believed it, of course," the girl said. "They'd have thought you off your head." She gave Melody a brief glance and then fixed her eyes back on the road. She drove well. It was hard to imagine her doing anything badly. "Have you got enough money for your ticket?"

She got her answer from Melody's face. She'd not given that a thought.

"I'll give it to you," she said. "I can collect it off Glenn later."

"You'll tell him you helped me?"

"I think he'll understand there was little else I could do under the circumstances. If I'd had time to think, or had any warning, I think I would have left you where you were. But as it was . . . Well . . ." She shrugged her shoulders. "He'll be able to cope even if I have set him back a little. Glenn is an expert in handling emergencies. You'll be doing the explaining, no doubt."

"If he has any sense he'll keep away from me."

She laughed. "You sound so fierce. I can almost picture Glenn shaking in his shoes. Only he's a tough man, infant child. He doesn't shake easily."

Melody stared out of the window. Infant child! She resented that. Kate was treating it almost as a joke now, but she *had* been kidnapped and Glenn couldn't have any other reason but the jewels.

He'd probably got the idea from what happened on Sunday—seen it as a way to get rich quick.

"What did I say that made you stop asking questions?" she said abruptly and swung round to catch any telltale signs from Kate's face. But she merely raised her eyebrows. "I don't know what you mean."

"In the cottage . . . you were asking me how I'd met Glenn and when I told you it seemed to give you a shock."

"Nonsense. What's so shocking about meeting Glenn through your job?"

"That's what I was wondering."

She shook her head from side to side. "I can't understand your being suspicious of me. Am I not doing everything I can to help you?"

"Yes." Melody sank back into her seat. She was. She would probably be still locked up in the cottage if Kate hadn't come along. She had to be imagining that peculiar look. Kate had been as frank as an open book.

She had nearly an hour to wait for a

train. Kate bought her ticket and waited with her.

"Give Glenn my love," she said as the whistle blew. "And you'd better tell him I'll be at the cottage for the next three weeks—just in case."

Melody had resisted the impulse to ask —several times over—but she couldn't bite it back any longer.

"Just *who* are you?"

"You looked in my handbag. Did I come back too soon?" She smiled wickedly at Melody's spreading flush. "I'm precise in my habits. You put my passport back in a different position."

"I wasn't going to deny it," Melody said stiffly. "After all you did the same thing to me. But knowing your name doesn't exactly answer my question. You called him yours."

"*My* Glenn!" Her eyes gleamed with laughter. "Does it bother you then?"

Melody pulled up the window quite viciously and went to her seat. She could see that smile and the gleam in Kate's eyes long after the train had left the station.

She had to be a girl friend. He'd said he had no family. And besides her name was quite different. And yet any normal girl friend would surely have displayed a more hostile attitude in finding her as she did. Locked in or not.

She tried to stop thinking about it. That sort of thinking was stupid. She had to sort out what she would say to the police instead, for, of course, her father would have brought them in again.

Maybe they'd even managed to do some investigating this time. She went to the buffet for a snack. She didn't think they'd have stirred themselves much. But they would certainly want to hear her story.

She got a sausage roll and a cup of coffee, finding to her surprise that she was absolutely ravenous. She had a sandwich too and then decided to wait until she got home. There'd be something better to eat there. But first her story . . . She had to get that right.

She went back to her seat. It was

always wise to stick to as much of the truth as possible. That way it would be hard for anyone to trip her up. Anyone? She realised with a sense of shock that she intended to keep her father and Aunt Prudence out of it too. No one was to know about the cottage belonging to Glenn—at least not until she'd seen him first. Maybe he had some explanation. Maybe he could prove it couldn't possibly have been him. Someone could be using him, as her father had been used. She couldn't judge him without a hearing.

The train pulled into the station and she stood up and made her way to the door.

She'd wanted to see Glenn before anyone else and it looked as if she was going to get her wish. He was standing near the ticket barrier.

She pulled her head back in at once and stood perfectly still, her heart beating fast.

She wanted to see him, to talk to him, to find out the truth. But not here, where

she could be whisked off and hidden away
again.

She'd listen to him yes, but with her
family around her where she was safe.
And she realised to her horror how much
afraid of him she was.

8

THE other passengers filed past her, some showing their annoyance at the obstruction that hindered their progress, others noticing nothing, intent only on getting off the train and completing their journey.

When the last one had gone she relaxed from her taut position pressed in against the corridor wall and quietly slid into the toilet compartment.

They were at the end of the line. The cleaners would descend any moment to clean up the litter. There would be half an hour, maybe more, before the train began to fill with people again and return to London.

Glenn couldn't know for certain she was on this train. He would be meeting them all, anxious to get hold of her before anyone else had a chance to talk to her, anxious to find out what she knew.

She waited, giving him time to assure himself she wasn't on this train. He wouldn't wait continuously on the platform. He'd be in the bar, whiling the hours away with coffee or something stronger, going out only when the trains from London were due.

The cleaners arrived en masse, calling out to one another, stoically cheerful at the mess that waited for them. She tensed but no one tried the door.

When all was silent again she stepped out of the toilet and cautiously went to the door, peering towards the barrier.

The ticket inspector was just changing the board there. He took up his position and started to allow the people through. There was no sign of Glenn.

Melody descended and walked steadily up the platform.

The inspector regarded her in surprise. "What happened to you then?"

"I fell asleep." She met his gaze stonily.

He opened his mouth and then shrugged and let her pass. She could feel him watching her as she walked towards the taxi rank and hoped Glenn didn't strike up a conversation with him the next time he came out. But it didn't matter if he did. She would be home by then.

In a little under half an hour she was in her father's arms.

They were all there, even Tom. She had barely paid the taxi off before they were streaming out of the house to welcome her.

She held her hands up in protest, smiling and laughing at the barrage of questions that were being fired at her from all sides. "One at a time, please. I'm fine, truly I am. Don't all look so worried."

"Come inside. What are we doing, standing out here in the cold!" Her father drew her along the path, reluctant to release his hold on her. "Have you been hurt? What happened? We—"

"No questions," Natalie interrupted firmly. "Wait. Can't you see the poor child is nearly at the end of her tether. She's as white as a sheet."

"Are you hungry?" Aunt Prudence cried. "Have you eaten?"

"I could eat now," Melody said.

"So could we all," Michael declared. "And maybe now we'll get the chance."

"Oh dear, Michael! Have they been starving you?" Melody laughed. She was feeling lightheaded in the relief at being home again.

"It's all very well for you," Michael said darkly. "You've not been wondering and worrying about what could have happened to you. A fellow loses his appetite when he's imagining the worst. Even after you phoned no one could relax. We kept thinking something else could happen to you."

"Well, nothing has," she said lightly. "Here I am. All in one piece. I was very careful."

"You should have been careful before. How *could* you let yourself be taken again?"

"Michael!" her father exclaimed sharply. "We all know how concerned you've been but just let your sister catch

230

her breath. We can wait to hear what happened."

"Maybe you can." Michael was unabashed and even in this moment of stress Melody notice and rejoiced at the way he smiled at his father. A week ago she wouldn't have believed it possible. His smile turned on her. "If I have to wait much longer I'll explode."

Melody laughed and sat down on the couch. "All right, Michael. I'll put you out of your misery."

"Wait a minute—where's Glenn?" Natalie cried. "He was to meet you at the station. He's been there for hours."

"He must have missed me in the crowd," Melody said carelessly.

"I can't imagine him doing that." Natalie turned to Tom. "You'd better go and tell him Melody is home again."

"He'll be so relieved," Aunt Prudence said. "He took the news of your disappearance badly."

"Really?" Melody raised her eyebrows. "When did he find out about it?"

"He returned from London last night

231

and came straight to see you." Aunt Prudence met Melody's eyes steadily. "You were hurt I know, at the way he left without a word. But don't spoil things by pretending indifference now. He cares about you. He couldn't hide it."

Melody lowered her eyes swiftly. If her aunt did but know. Indifference! More a burning bitterness. He could act. It must have been quite a moving performance to convince Aunt Prudence.

"What did he do?"

"Never mind about him," Michael said in exasperation. "What about you?"

"Well, it was like this." Melody settled herself more comfortably and told how she had been kidnapped, sticking strictly to the truth until the moment when she opened her eyes and found herself in the little room. "There was everything I could possibly need," she said. "It looked as if I was meant to stay there for weeks. The window was boarded over and the door would have kept a regiment in. I concentrated on the window. It took me a long time but I got the boards away and then I smashed the glass and climbed out by knotting the sheets together. It was a big old house set in a wilderness of a garden but there wasn't a soul around. I walked for hours, sticking to the fields. I thought it was safer. Then I came to a main road and hitched a lift from a London bound lorry. After that it was easy. I phoned you from a petrol station when the driver stopped for a few minutes. I didn't tell him I'd been kidnapped, of course. He might have thought I'd escaped from a mental home or something."

"Could you find the house again?" her father demanded.

She shook her head, finding she couldn't meet his eyes. "I don't honestly know where I was except that it must have been somewhere down south. It was deep in the heart of the country; there were woods and little lanes, isolated farms. I could have gone to one of those, I suppose, but it would have sounded so ridiculous to tell them my story. I was sure no one would believe me. I looked for signposts but didn't see any." Changing the subject before she could involve herself in something that gave her away she said, "Don't you think it odd that you had no demand? That they didn't try to contact you at all?"

"I thought that at first," her father said soberly. "But I can vouch for it being a successful softening up process. If I'd only had the jewels I'd have had them ready to hand over at the first word. In fact, I was . . . well, no matter."

"What? What did you think? No!" Melody laid her hand on his arm and gazed into her father's eyes earnestly. "You can't do that. Not ever." She saw by his expression that she'd read his intention correctly. But she'd known it. She'd been afraid of it. He'd do anything for her. "I'd sooner die than know my father was a thief," she said passionately. "I believe in you. You've always to believe in me. Hold on to your principles. Things will always work out if you do that."

His expression didn't change. He was

unconvinced. She said quickly, "You went to the police, I suppose? What did they do?"

"Nothing!" Natalie said explosively. "Absolutely nothing. They seemed convinced you'd gone off on your own accord. They said— Well never mind what they said. That note you left, Melody . . . You've not explained that. Why did you write it?"

"It was a draft, actually," Melody said. "I got to thinking about what you said. I thought a new job would be a very good thing for me. But I'd have worked out my notice. Surely Mr. Travis didn't think I'd just walked out?"

"Heaven knows what that man thinks," Natalie said in disgust. "I talked to him myself this morning and couldn't get any sense out of him at all. Now we know why. He helped them. He wrote the note that got you down in the basement."

"No, I don't think so," Melody said slowly. "It was typewritten. Anyone could have done it."

"And how many people know the intricacies of your filing system?" Natalie demanded shrewdly.

Glenn knew. He'd have found out. And did Mr. Travis suspect something? He had to. But he was too afraid of what Glenn could do to his job to voice his fears. "I don't think Mr. Travis would be party to any crime," Melody said after a pause. "He wouldn't have the stomach for it."

"He knows something," Natalie asserted positively. "I told the police that but they laughed in my face. I don't know when I've been so angry. I could have slapped Bolton across the ears. They thought I was a silly, hysterical woman with too much money and they were so intent on putting me in my place that they didn't listen to a word I said."

"I'll talk to Mr. Travis tomorrow."

Four aghast faces stared at her. It was Michael who voiced the collective thought. "You're not intending to go back to work again, are you?"

"Why not?"

"But you can't."

"I'll work out my notice," she said stubbornly. "And I'll get the truth out of Mr. Travis if I have to beat him over the head for it."

"Now don't do anything foolish," Aunt Prudence said nervously.

"He's afraid of something. I know that already. A man like that doesn't go to pieces for nothing."

"He knows about me," her father said heavily. "Natalie found out that much."

"It's true," Natalie said. "He had your letter of resignation and in some way it seemed to give him comfort. He kept fingering it and saying it was the best way out. I told you he didn't make sense. Melody . . ." Her voice softened. "I got the feeling he'd been going to fire you. Don't go back. It could be humiliating."

She could be right. Mr. Travis's embarrassment and nervousness could be due to the fact that Glenn had told him about her father and he knew he would have to tell her to go, hating himself because he had to do it.

But she wanted facts not suppositions.

She would go to see him. Tomorrow. "He can't eat me," she said aloud. "I'll see him if only to confirm my resignation."

"Then I'll go with you," Natalie announced.

"All right." She accepted it for the moment. Time enough when they got there to insist on seeing Mr. Travis alone. She would have to make sure Glenn was out of the way too and at the thought she wondered why he hadn't stopped Natalie talking to Mr. Travis. Was he so sure that he had him frightened into silence?

"Why did you go to see Mr. Travis?" she said casually. "Couldn't Glenn have talked to him?"

"I dare say. I was in such a state I wasn't thinking straight. It was a dreadful night. Tom waited over half an hour for you before he decided something was wrong. He went in the building and could find no one there but the cleaners. He called me and I phoned the police right away. It was hours before we heard anything from them and then they came up with your letter of resignation and said you'd probably got scared and run off to a safe hiding place. As if you'd have done that without telling us! I was *so* mad."

Melody laughed at her indignant face. "Well, all's well that end's well."

"But is it ended?" her father said bitterly. "I'd better call the police and tell them you're back."

"Why bother!" Aunt Prudence said heavily.

"We won't give them any lever to use against us. If this goes on . . ." Her father didn't complete the sentence but moved with bowed shoulders to the phone.

A look of dismay was exchanged between the two older women and Michael bit his lip.

"It won't happen again," Melody said firmly. "I'll make sure of that. Now didn't someone mention food? It's a long time coming up."

Aunt Prudence took her cue and managed to sound cheerful. "It won't take a minute. How about a mixed grill?"

"Anything," Michael said fervently.

"Anything!" He took her arm. "I'll even help you and make sure you're not distracted by anything else."

Aunt Prudence cast her eyes up high. "The heavens preserve us. Charred sausage and cindered steak on the way."

"Don't be cheeky." Michael led her firmly into the kitchen and Natalie murmured, "I'll see what I can do too," and tactfully left Melody alone with her father.

"They're coming round," he said, turning away from the phone. "I suppose they have to make a token gesture even for a hardened criminal."

"Don't let them upset you," Melody said gently. "It's not worth it."

"I feel so helpless. All I could do was sit by the phone. Waiting and worrying . . . without the reassurance that the police were working for us. A man forfeits so many things with just one mistake. If only I'd left that necklace alone."

"You can't change the past. It's the future you look to now. Something will

240

happen. They'll find out you weren't the thief. Believe that, father, please."

He smiled faintly and came to sit beside her, his arm sliding round her shoulders. "What would I do without you?"

"You'll do nothing wrong. Promise me that."

He didn't answer for a moment and then he moved away.

"I'd commit murder for you," he said bleakly. "If I get my hands on the person who's behind these kidnap attempts I couldn't promise anything."

Melody's heart missed a beat. Two kinds of fear tied her tongue in knots—fear that her father meant what he said and fear for Glenn. Supposing he gave himself away when he saw her? What would her father do?

"I've not been hurt," she said carefully. "But if you took the law into your own hands it can only result in tragedy. Besides, that's not what I meant."

"I know what you meant," he said with a sigh. "But I don't see any way out. How can I convince these people I don't have

the jewels? Can I sit back and let them
. . . allow them to ill-treat you? Don't you
see how impossible the situation is? It
would be better if I were back in jail. At
least you would be safe then."

"No! Don't think like that." Melody
sprang up and clutched her father's arm.
She gazed imploringly into his face.
"You've got to have faith."

"In what?" Her father's mouth twisted
painfully.

"In me. In all of us."

He looked down at her but before he
could speak the doorbell rang. "That will
be the police. I'll let them in."

It was the same pair; the cadaverous
Bolton and his hard-eyed second-in-
command.

Glenn arrived as she was halfway
through her story. He came into the
room, carefully shutting the door behind
him. After one glance Melody didn't look
at him again. The police made no objection to his presence. She wished they did.
It was difficult to go on with the story,
even more difficult to retain her

composure as Bolton fixed his eyes on her and fired the inevitable questions.

He didn't believe her. He made that obvious. So she couldn't give a good description of the house in which she had been imprisoned? Big and square . . . what sort of description was that? And she hadn't found out where she was? Incredible! And how convenient to hit on a lorry driver who could take her into London, asking no questions which might embarrass her. She wouldn't know his name of course . . . or the firm he worked for. She wouldn't even have noticed what he was carrying.

"I dare say that if anyone else had been through what I'd been through they wouldn't be in a state of mind to notice things either," Melody said hotly. "Descriptions! It didn't seem to inspire you much when you had them in abundance. What have you found out about those first two men. Who were *they* working for? Did you even bother to try to find out? All right! You've made the gesture of doing your duty. You can go back to the station and report you don't believe a word I've said. I don't care what you do. You're worse than hopeless anyway."

Bolton didn't say a word. He rose to his feet and they left the room without a backward glance.

No one moved to show them out. Glenn shut the door behind them and waited behind it as if ready to open it again.

"I'll go and see how that mixed grill is coming along," her father said taking the hint a little belatedly.

"They won't want you in there," Melody said quickly. "The kitchen's overcrowded as it is." She still didn't look at Glenn.

Her father glanced from her to Glenn uncertainly. He had to find some excuse to leave. He could feel the tension mounting minute by minute. "I think I'd better tell them the police have gone," he said firmly.

Glenn slanted a smile at him, wafting

him through the door with alacrity, but the smile went as soon as he'd gone.

Melody could feel his eyes upon her. He stood leaning against the door in an almost casual stance but there was nothing casual about his intention. She knew why he stayed there.

"Don't worry about anyone walking in and hearing something they shouldn't," she said tartly. "They think I'm upset because you went off to London so abruptly and they'll give us plenty of time to kiss and make up."

"Is that what you want?"

"Don't be ridiculous," she said disdainfully.

"You saw me at the station, didn't you? You must have deliberately avoided me."

"Don't tell me you wonder why?"

"But I do wonder. Why not enlighten me?"

"You don't really think I was such a fool as I made out to the police? I knew where I was. I could have given them a very accurate description of that cottage and then gone on to give the name of the village those few miles down the road."

"What stopped you?"

The last lingering hope that had persisted in spite of everything died an acrid death. "You know why," she said in a low voice. "You must have banked on that. How else would you have the nerve to come back here and face me? How could you do it, Glenn? How could you have put my family through all that misery and dread?"

"It wouldn't have been for long."

"How do you count time? Every minute must have seemed like an eternity to my father. You'd have driven him to steal. He felt he had to have something to offer."

"I made no demands."

"You didn't have to, did you? He knew why I'd been taken and you'd stocked that room with enough food for a month. He'd have gone crazy within a week."

"I don't think so, but it was a risk I had to take. Your safety came first."

"My *safety*?" She stared at him

incredulously. "You're not going to tell me you kidnapped me for my own good! That the thought of getting the jewels never crossed your mind?"

"I was thinking mainly of you. Whoever was behind that kidnap attempt would have tried again—will *try* again. You should have stayed where you were. You were safe."

"And why didn't you tell my father that? I may be fool enough to have fallen in love with you but it doesn't addle my brain. You want those jewels, don't you?"

He held her gaze steadily and then said softly, "If you really believe in your father's innocence you'll trust me."

"You mean keep quiet about what you've done? You must think I'm a complete lunatic."

"If your father is innocent I'll prove it."

"Would you mind telling me how," she said through her teeth.

"I can't tell you that. But I must be on hand, accepted. To be turned out of this house now could mean the end of the hope of your father ever being freed from the suspicion and doubt that surrounds him. Are you willing to take that chance?"

He was conning her, using the one weapon that couldn't fail. She stared at him. Trust him! He'd said that before and look what had happened. And now he thought he could make a fool of her again. He stood there—smooth, assured, confident that he could make her do as he wanted. Suddenly she hated him.

"We don't need you. We'll prove it ourselves."

"You mean Natalie's little scheme? It might work—but then again it might not. Gadgets have a habit of going wrong. I'd be added insurance. I've got friends. I've found out something which might interest you. Those two men were working for Hartley."

"How did you find that out?"

"Questions . . . answers . . . money changing hands. You can find out a lot if you know where to go and who to ask. It had to be someone who knew where you were. That meant it was almost certain to be someone at the party. Hartley was an obvious first choice to start working on."

"But those men could have followed us there. My father thought someone was following us when we left the prison."

"A man thinks the whole world is watching him when he comes out of jail but no one followed your father to Natalie's, nor us. I would have noticed."

"Have you told the police?"

"I've no proof—and that's not really what I'm after. The only reason I'm telling you is that it's a sample of what I can find out and also I'd like to put you on your guard. You might think you can trust Hartley because he's a friend of Natalie's."

"You've got to be joking."

"Then you wouldn't go anywhere with him whatever reason he might come up with?"

"I wouldn't go *anywhere* with *anyone* at the moment."

"Good. I'm going to suggest I stay the

night here. I can bed down on the couch."

"You're very sure I'm not going to tell my father about you, aren't you?"

"Am I wrong?"

She held his gaze. "I'll not say anything —not at the moment. But I'm going to write down what really happened and leave it at the bank. If anything else happens to me they'll know who is responsible. You won't get away with it again."

Laughter glinted in his eyes. "A wise decision. Make sure, however, that someone is appointed to notify the bank if you disappear. It could be years before they find out otherwise."

"I'm not a child," she said stiffly. "So don't keep treating me like one. If you imagine you've gulled me completely you can think again. I know you're not concerned about my safety, or with proving my father's innocence. You didn't answer my question but you didn't have to. I know you want the jewels. You think if you can get close to my father you'll find out where they are—even without the pressure of my disappearance acting on him. That's what you've got in mind, isn't it?"

He straightened up. There was an almost imperceptible pause and then he said deliberately, "That's what I had in mind; yes."

She looked away from him. How cold he seemed. Cold and calculating. A suspicion confirmed by his own words. She'd expected him to deny it; she'd wanted him to deny it.

"You won't get the jewels," she said in a hard voice, "but you'll find out what a truly decent and honest person he is. Maybe you'll learn something from him."

"Melody . . ." He stepped forward and then checked himself as Michael put his head round the door. "Aunt Prudence wants to know if it's all right to lay the table."

"Of course it is," Melody said at once, not knowing whether to be glad or sorry at the interruption. If he wondered whether his admission would make any difference to her promise to keep silent let him stew about it.

Michael came in with the cloth and a handful of cutlery. "You're staying, Glenn?"

"As a matter of fact," Glenn said as Melody's father came in on Michael's heels. "I thought it might be a good idea to bed down here for the next few nights."

"A good idea," Aunt Prudence said in approval carrying in a steaming platter.

"Yes, yes," her father agreed but Melody noticed the momentary hesitation and knew Glenn had too. He'd put it down to a guilty conscience, of course. Not the natural doubts of a man who wasn't master in the house in which he was living.

"I can take Melody into work too," Glenn added.

"I'm not going back," Melody said quietly.

"Why not?"

She didn't look at him. "Maybe you can think of a reason."

"You don't think—" Natalie began and stopped.

"I think whoever gets landed with that rotten old typewriter is the most unfortunate of creatures," Melody said lightly and carefully refraining from looking at anyone in particular began to pull out the chairs.

What kind of perverse streak was this? First to hit out and then to protect? "I'll be surprised if she lasts out longer than the first day." She glanced round the table and paused as if only then seeing the effect of her words. "Oh, I wasn't accusing Glenn of having been the one who told Mr. Travis," She said. "He wouldn't do that. I told him it might cost me my job." She smiled at Glenn. "And you told me I could trust you. Remember?"

"I remember." Glenn returned her smile easily but it didn't extend to his eyes. She had got through to him. He added, "And I didn't tell him."

She let the doubt show on her face but

only to him. She'd find out tomorrow. When she saw Mr. Travis.

Before she left that night Natalie arranged to pick her up when Aunt Prudence left for school. She had no intention of leaving Melody alone for an instant. "If they try to take you again, they'll have me to reckon with," she declared. "And if that doesn't make them think twice I've got one or two things up my sleeve to convince them."

She decided they would make Mr. Travis the first call of the day but when they got there the secretary told them he wouldn't be available all morning.

Something in her manner told Melody their visit had been expected. Glenn again. She'd tried hard to steer the conversation away from her intention of the morning but it had come out inevitably when Natalie had taken her departure.

"We'll wait," she told the girl, nudging Natalie as she opened her mouth to protest.

"All morning?" the girl exclaimed. "Wouldn't it be wiser to come back?"

"I don't think so." After half an hour of two pairs of eyes watching her every movement, the girl's nerves began to fray at the edges. "It really isn't the slightest use waiting," she said after her third attempt to type a letter had gone into the waste paper basket.

"You're going to have to leave this office some time," Melody said pleasantly. "And then I'll walk past your desk and through into that office you're guarding so zealously. Why don't you take your break now? Otherwise you're going to be working overtime catching up with yourself."

"I'll be in trouble."

"No, you won't. You've not told Mr. Travis we're out here waiting. We could have just arrived."

"You won't tell him?"

"Wouldn't dream of it."

"I'm off then."

"Stay out here," Melody told Natalie. "Make sure we're not interrupted."

"I'm coming in with you."

"No, Natalie. You keep guard. There's no other door. I'll be quite safe. Mr. Travis wouldn't hurt a fly."

She went into the office and closed the door behind her. Mr. Travis wasn't at his desk. He was over by the window staring blindly through the glass. "Sit down, Melody," he said without looking around. "I've been expecting you."

"Really? Did Glenn tell you I was back?"

"Glenn!"

She was shocked at the amount of loathing he put into the name, and even more shocked at his appearance when he turned round. He was haggard and sunken-eyed.

"I can battle with my conscience no longer. I'm going to tell you about that man. He's a fake, Melody. No more an O and M expert than you are. But they made me be a party to the whole thing and I was afraid of losing my job. Sit down. I think this is going to be something of a shock for you but I have to tell you."

9

MELODY sat down. She felt no
emotion, not even surprise.

"He's an insurance investi-
gator," Mr. Travis said. "One of the best.
He's never fallen down on a job yet.
Maybe you don't know, Melody, but this
company insured those jewels for Mrs.
Galbreith. They had to pay out a lot of
money and they want it back. Head Office
hired Glenn Hunter and he found out
right away that you were employed here.
It made it easy for him. Your father
would have been suspicious of any ordinary stranger making a sudden play for
you, trying to ingratiate himself within
the family but the way he played it
Hunter made it the most natural thing in
the world. I believe he has a flair for
turning situations to his advantage. He's
tough and smart and without scruples.

"I didn't like it, Melody. I tried to fight

it. I told them it wasn't ethical to use you in such a way but the individual doesn't matter to them. Only the end result. I was told what I had to do and I didn't have any choice. Only when he arrived I knew you would be hurt. He's the type of man who hurts girls like you without even trying."

Melody remembered that first morning she had met Glenn. She had known then —the way he looked at her. He'd marked her down as a victim. And she had made it so easy for him. Despite that warning intuition she had gone right along the lines he intended.

She wished now that Michael hadn't interrupted the night before. Glenn might have carried on and told her the whole truth. He couldn't prefer her to believe he was an opportunist who had suddenly seen a way of reaching the easy life.

She stared blindly at the immaculate blotter on the desk and knew she was reaching out for false hopes again. Mr. Travis hadn't done a stroke of work that morning. Glenn had warned him not to talk to her. He was afraid if she knew the whole truth she would tell her father. He had deceived her from the start and he would go on deceiving her until he no longer had any need of her.

"I appreciate your telling me, Mr. Travis," she said sombrely.

"I don't suppose . . ." He hesitated and then said with a rush, "If you could see your way to keeping it quiet I would be very grateful."

She looked at him, knowing the effort it had cost for him to tell her and knowing too that he hated asking her for her silence. Maybe he guessed the effort it would take. "I won't tell anyone," she said, and she rose. "Goodbye, Mr. Travis. I don't suppose I'll be seeing you again."

He got to his feet awkwardly. "I've got your cards here and a month's salary. I'm sorry about all this, Melody. I'd grown very fond of you and I think you have the makings of a good secretary. If you want a reference at any time, don't hesitate to ask."

"No, I won't." She slipped the envelope he handed her into her bag and shook his proffered hand. "Goodbye."

He was back at the window when she left the office. Well, he'd sleep better now. He'd eased his conscience. Poor Mr. Travis. She felt almost as sorry for him as she did for herself. She was going to have to act a lie now. There was no one she could tell. Glenn would sense any change in attitude towards him. Her family weren't good at hiding their feelings.

"Well?" Natalie demanded, rising to her feet impatiently.

It was pointless considering telling Natalie either. She might be able to act but she wouldn't see the need for it. She hadn't liked Mr. Travis.

"It wasn't Glenn who told him about father," Melody said through stiff lips. "He knew before Glenn arrived." She could hear herself asking Glenn not to say anything. It was like rubbing salt into an open wound. He'd let her believe in him, maybe with a few momentary qualms but not enough to divert him from his goal. Mr. Travis had known all this time. And Head Office knew. They had used her like a pawn on a chessboard. Glenn had probably known that when this was all over she would be sacked. At least, she had saved herself the ignominy of that.

She tried to thrust the whole thing to the back of her mind and smiled brightly at Natalie. "I've got a month's salary and I feel like buying a new dress. Let's go."

The day passed; a peculiar day in which thoughts of Glenn persisted in weaving a pattern between the preparations for the catching of a thief.

They lunched with the friend whose jewels Natalie was using as bait and in the afternoon Natalie took her own necklace in.

Miles was in the shop showing some rings to an overdressed woman but as soon as he saw and recognised Natalie he hurried over, his teeth flashing in his most winning smile.

Melody waited in the background watching his performance dispassionately.

Urbane, polished, immaculately groomed; presenting a flawless picture of a gentleman whose integrity was beyond question. She could see him on the stand —the loyal friend who couldn't believe in her father's guilt. It had to be him. Somehow he'd got away with the jewels. But he had been sitting on them, afraid to unload them—that was why he had wanted her father back.

Natalie handled him in a masterly fashion. No one could have guessed what she thought of the man in reality. Her charm poured over him, sweet and smooth and as thick as honey, and he lapped it all up, expanding visibly under the treatment with only one setback when he said that Ford would of course see to a new catch on the necklace.

"*Mr.* Ford." Natalie's tone froze him for that moment and then he was smiling again as Natalie hastened to cover up her involuntary reaction by offering an excuse in the form of Melody. "You'll remember his daughter, I expect."

His gaze went beyond Natalie, his smile

faltering as he met the open antagonism on Melody's face, but then he rallied. "How could I forget Melody! The memory of last time we met has haunted me." He came forward, taking her limp, unwilling hand in his. "I'm sorry I couldn't do more, sorry it turned out as it did. But it's over now. If your father and I can be friends again I'm sure we can too."

Melody could sense Natalie's flashing signals, the demand to be pleasant and amiable, to lull him into a state of false security, but she couldn't do it. She would make a mess of it and then Miles might wonder why she was making the effort and grow suspicious.

She removed her hand, smiled thinly and said that some things could never be forgotten.

The disconcerted Miles was rescued by Natalie and he turned to her in undisguised relief and thereafter ignored Melody.

"You shouldn't have behaved like that," Natalie scolded as they came out of the shop. "I can't stand him either but I didn't show it."

"It was necessary for you not to show it—not me. I couldn't do it, Natalie. I'm sorry, but I'm not a good actress."

"You needn't tell me that," Natalie said, climbing into the Rolls and directing Tom to the hairdresser's. "You've been as blue devilled as I don't-know-what despite your efforts to hide it. What really happened this morning? What did that man Travis tell you?"

"I can't tell you, Natalie. I promised. It might cost him his job."

"It's something to do with that young man of yours, isn't it? What is he? A special investigator?"

Melody's jaw dropped.

"I'm not devoid of brains," Natalie said complacently. "There are some very odd qualities about Glenn and I did wonder when I talked to Mr. Travis. I know how these companies work. I'm right, aren't I?"

Melody nodded dumbly.

"I suppose his idea was to get to know

you well enough to be accepted by your father. It's far easier to watch someone as a friend of the family than trying to be an invisible shadow. He must be congratulating himself—you've fallen in love with him and he's spending a lot of time in your home. He couldn't do any better than that, could he?"

Melody murmured a strangled, "No," and Natalie patted her hand kindly. "Don't make a tragedy of it. He might come in useful. His word will carry a lot of weight."

"You won't let him know that you've guessed about him, will you?"

Natalie cocked her eyebrow. "Because of Travis? It doesn't do to be too soft, my dear, but I'll keep quiet. It's an ace up our sleeves."

"He believes in father's guilt."

"Well now . . . I don't think he's as sure about that as he was," Natalie said thoughtfully. "How are you going to hide what you feel about him?"

"He—well, I—There's reason enough to explain a difference in my attitude to him. He told me last night he meant to get the jewels. You see—" She took a deep breath. "He kidnapped me that second time."

Natalie's eyes grew round. "But—" she began and then changed her mind. "You knew this? Last night?"

"Yes."

"When you talked to us?"

"Yes."

"And the police?"

Melody nodded. "Don't tell me what you think of me," she said miserably.

"Well!" Natalie exclaimed and was silent for a moment before saying curiously, "Did he have second thoughts and let you go?"

"Oh no. He'd envisaged every possibility but his girlfriend turning up unexpectedly at the cottage where he'd put me. She thought it all a joke. She's an air hostess, very beautiful—just the type you'd imagine he'd pick. Her name is Kate."

"Oh dear," Natalie murmured. "Very beautiful?"

"*Very.*"

"That's a pity."

"Why?" Melody said belligerently. "You don't imagine I could possibly care for him at all after what he's done to me. He can have as many beautiful girls as he wants."

"But you covered up for him," Natalie pointed out blandly.

"Well . . ." She made an irritable gesture with her shoulders. "He might have had some explanation."

"And did he?"

"He said he'd been concerned about my safety."

"How very noble of him. He couldn't inform us what he'd done though. He was waiting for your father to crack, I suppose."

"I thought so."

"Unscrupulous," Natalie murmured. "And yet you still didn't tell your father afterwards."

"My father has nothing to be afraid of. Glenn can watch him as much as he likes."

"You see what I mean about him coming in useful." Natalie leaned back, her voice as smooth as silk. "I have to confess to a certain admiration for the man. You know, I was the one to tell him you'd got away. It must have given him quite a shock and yet he managed to sound as if I'd given him a million dollar present. And last night . . . Coming back to face you, wondering what you knew, wondering if the police were going to arrest him . . . He's got guts."

"I would call it conceit."

"Would you, my dear?" Natalie smiled. "But then you're angry with him now. You think he had no right to deceive you—that's the thing that rankles most, isn't it?"

"I'm not a person to him, just someone to be used and manipulated." She thought of Aunt Prudence using almost the same words. She had seen through Glenn but the kidnapping he had arranged had won her over, or rather the way he had acted when they had all been under stress.

"You might be right." Natalie was agreeing with infuriating placidity. "Does he know how you got away?"

"No."

"Uhm." Natalie's smile became positively saint-like. "I'd like to be there when he finds out. It might jolt his complacency a little."

"What do you mean?"

Natalie lifted her hands expressively. "Don't let it bother you. We don't want to rock the boat yet awhile."

"Now listen to me, Natalie," Melody said explosively.

"Get this straight once and for all. I've no more interest in Glenn Hunter other than as a man who might be able to help my father. I don't give a hoot who helped me to get away. She could have been a charwoman for all I cared."

"If you say so, dear." Natalie had the maddening air of one who knew better but refused to argue about it. "How are you going to have your hair done?"

She didn't care how she had her hair done and she said so but Natalie only laughed and refused to return to the topic of Glenn.

They were nearly two hours at the hairdressers and while they were there Tom picked up Michael and brought him in to wait for them. Then there was just time to go back to Natalie's flat and allow her to change before they went to the shop.

A hold up in the traffic made them a few minutes later than Natalie had intended. The staff were just leaving and there was no sign of Miles.

Melody's father was surprised to see them. They hadn't told him they were going to meet him.

"Has Miles gone?" Natalie asked, glancing around casually.

"Yes, he left early."

"And asked you to lock up?" Natalie exchanged a significant glance with Melody. "But you're not on your own, are you?"

"No. We've got a new secretary." Peter lowered his voice. "Something of an eager beaver. As soon as Miles left she decided it was a good time to clear out the cupboards in my room. I've not had a minute's peace. Talk! I wouldn't have believed anyone could go on so long and now, of course, she's got everything out of the cupboards and won't leave until she's put it all back. I think I'm going to be here for another hour by the look of it."

"Oh, I expect she'll have finished by now." Natalie walked through into the main office followed by a curious Melody.

She didn't quite know what to expect but nothing in her mind's eye prepared her for the sight of the beaded, shingled grey-haired figure; almost a caricature of the flapper girl of the twenties, angular and ungainly. No one in the wildest flights of their imagination could suspect this woman of being a private detective. She looked foolish and even a little stupid, but she needed only a glance at Natalie and within five minutes what had looked like a colossal mess on the floor was neatly stowed away in the cupboards.

"I've finished now, Mr. Ford," she said

breathlessly. "I'm sorry I've been so long."

"It's all right. Don't worry about it."

"Goodnight then." As she passed Melody their eyes met. The false eyelashes fluttered, she could have sworn there was a ghost of a wink and then she had minced from the room leaving a scent of cheap perfume behind her.

"A very odd woman," her father murmured with a shake of his head, looking at the neat cupboards in disbelief.

"Never mind her," Natalie said gaily. "Let's go." The first step was accomplished. Peter hadn't been left alone in his office for even a fleeting second. There'd been no opportunity for him to take anything out of the safe and they had someone to swear to it.

He put on his coat, hesitating, glancing uncertainly around the room. "I feel there's something wrong."

"Such as what?" Natalie met his eyes with innocence.

"I don't know." He was frowning. "Maybe because this afternoon was almost a repetition of the afternoon before I was arrested. We've got some jewels in, worth almost as much as yours, Natalie. And then Miles brought your necklace in. You didn't tell me about it."

"It slipped my mind." She continued to meet his gaze with the same limpid innocence. "Does it bother you?"

"I'm surprised you trusted us for a second time," he said slowly.

"Heavens, Peter! Let's not go into that again. You would have been upset if I'd taken it somewhere else and I wasn't risking that."

"I'd have understood."

"That's the trouble with you. You understand too much. Would you understand if I asked you to open the safe now and check my necklace is still there?"

He stared at her and then without a word went over to the safe and spun the dial of the combination lock, pulling open the big heavy door. There was room enough to hold a man but it was shelved and loaded with stock.

Natalie stepped beside him and Melody

peered over her shoulder. This hadn't been on the agenda. They had discussed it but decided it would seem too odd a request, making her father suspect what they were up to. But Natalie wasn't one to miss an opportunity. It had come up in a natural way.

"Your necklace," her father said to Natalie. He made no move to pick it up but merely pointed. Natalie was the one to lift the case and open it.

The necklace gleamed on the black velvet, seductive and alluring. Natalie stared at it for a moment and then snapped the case shut and returned it to the shelf. "And these others," she said. "Where are they? Could I look?"

"There." He pointed again.

Natalie went on her knees and slid the big leather jewel case he indicated onto the floor.

Melody's breath caught in her throat as she opened the case. To own a collection of jewels like that meant riches indeed. Natalie's friend had favoured diamonds but there were emeralds too, and rubies and pearls. "Well, do they match yours, Natalie?" she said lightly.

Natalie lifted the top tray to reveal another collection of rings and bracelets. Her hand strayed to a solitaire fit for a queen. She checked herself and quickly replaced the tray, closing the case. "I'd give my eye teeth for that," she said frankly. "Put them away at once before the temptation gets too much for me."

Melody's father returned them in silence and closed the safe.

"Well," Natalie remarked brightly. "If history does repeat itself, you've got two witnesses to swear it was all locked up when you left the office this time."

"Is that why you did it?"

"One should take notice of premonitions." Natalie linked her arm through his. "I always do."

"Why did you pick me up tonight? Were you worried about your necklace?"

"Don't be silly." She urged him towards the door. "Michael is waiting in the car. He'll be wondering what has happened to us all."

"Yes." Melody added. "And if we're very much later then Aunt Prudence will start worrying. Is everything locked up?"

"I'll just set the alarm."

Before he got into the car he looked back, hesitating again. "I still have this feeling," he said.

"Relax, father. What can possibly be wrong?" Melody smiled at him but it brought him no comfort. Throughout the evening he was absent-minded and edgy. When the door bell went he stiffened and went at once to the window.

"It's only Glenn," Aunt Prudence told him. "He phoned to say he'd be late."

"Oh? Did he say why?" Melody demanded.

"We can't expect him to spend all his time here," Aunt Prudence said with some amusement.

Melody picked up the newspaper and rustled the pages irritably. She knew what her aunt was thinking but it wasn't like that. Not at all. All she'd wanted to know was whether he'd gone to his cottage. He'd want to check up on what damage she might have done in making her escape. And he'd have seen Kate.

She eyed him surreptitiously when he came in. He looked tired, but then with all the rushing about he'd been doing that week he had reason to be.

He sat down, stretching out his long legs, smiling at Aunt Prudence as she fussed around him, asking if he'd eaten, whether he'd like a drink. She could fix some sandwiches in a moment. Or perhaps something more substantial. It made Melody feel quite ill.

He settled for a sandwich and coffee and lit a cigarette while he was waiting for them. "Anything happen today? Where's Michael?"

"It's past ten. Use your powers of deduction."

Natalie directed a quelling glance at her, warned her to guard her tongue and followed on smoothly, telling Glenn there had been no incidents to the day and that now he was here she would take her departure.

Melody said, "Oh yes. We'll be safe

now with our guardian angel to watch over us. No need to worry any more." How could she guard her tongue, feeling as she did? Natalie had no right to tell her what to do.

"You talked to Travis?" Glenn said casually. He was drinking his coffee black.

"He gave me my cards and a month's salary." She got to her feet, unwilling to meet the probing stare that saw too much. "I'm going to bed. Goodnight, everyone."

She heard the Rolls drive off as she was undressing. A little later her aunt came up.

She lay in bed, consciously striving to stay awake.

The quiet rumble of conversation below seemed to go on for hours but at last her father came up to bed. She waited a little longer and then got up and went over to the window. Somewhere out there someone was watching the house, someone who would be able to swear her father had never left it. And downstairs Glenn lay on the couch. Her father would have to pass him to get out through the back door. He was protected on all sides and yet the unease he had been feeling all evening was transmitted to her.

The house was silent. It was past midnight. The avenue was equally quiet, the few lights in the neighbouring houses gradually quenched until by one o'clock all was dark.

Melody pulled on her dressing gown and silently opened her bedroom door. She would watch all night. She would be able to swear her father had never left his room.

She sat on the floor, her back to the wall. There wasn't a sound from downstairs. She wondered if Glenn was asleep. He'd had his coffee black. To help him stay awake?

She wished she'd had some. Her eyelids felt as heavy as lead. They kept closing despite her efforts. The temptation to lie on the floor was overwhelming.

She moved away from the wall. Even that uncompromising hardness offered an inducement to relax. Sitting crosslegged, her shoulders began to droop, her knees to ache. It was no use. She would have to stand. Impossible to fall asleep then, though after more long minutes she wasn't so sure.

She went to the window and opened it wide, thrusting her face into the cold wind and welcoming the freshness of the rain falling in a light drizzle. Not a nice night for anyone outside. She hoped Natalie's watcher was in a car and not huddled under a tree for shelter. How did they stay awake and watchful? How did anyone stay awake at night?

She stiffened. Something had moved out there in the darkness.

Her gaze roamed the garden; the shadows were black pools into which a man could melt and lose both shape and identity and then out of the corner of her eye she caught another movement and her gaze swivelled to the side of the house.

He came out of the shadows silently and with a suggestion of furtiveness in the way he looked around him. And then he was off, walking quickly, his head down, along the path and out through the garden gate. It wasn't Glenn. She'd have recognised him however dark it was. And somehow she didn't think it was Natalie's watcher either.

She checked her father's room, opening the door cautiously. His quiet, even breathing was reassuring.

But there wasn't a sound from the lounge. After a moment's hesitation she went inside. Somehow she felt the room was empty. There was a smell of cigarette smoke and of freshly made coffee.

She switched on the small table lamp. The couch was empty, the blankets neat. He hadn't even been lying on it.

Her glance ranged the room. He'd been sitting in the armchair, pulled up to the window. A thin stream of smoke came from a hastily dimped cigarette in the ash tray. She felt the coffee pot beside it. It was hot to the touch. There was a bottle of brandy too. He obviously had his ways of keeping awake. But where was he?

She checked the front door. The catch

was down, the chain fastened. But the back door was unbolted.

She went outside into the garden. The rain had grown heavier. She could feel it penetrating through her woollen dressing gown. She went back inside and changed her slippers for a pair of her aunt's old gardening shoes, pulling a macintosh over her head.

Glenn wasn't in the garden. She went out by the side path to the gate and looked up the avenue. Nothing moved but the rain, bouncing down on the gleaming roadway, rustling the trees. And then as she watched a man turned the corner at the far end of the avenue. He was walking swiftly, nothing stealthy in his movements.

She waited. It wasn't Glenn. His hair was dark and he had the bulk of middle age. He saw her watching him and checked for a moment. She thought he was going to come over but then he got into a car, sinking down into the seat. She wouldn't have known he was there if she hadn't seen him get in.

Natalie's watcher. And he quite definitely wasn't the man she had seen leaving their garden.

She turned back and looked at the house. What better way to implicate her father again than to plant something for the police to find. Had he tried to get into the house? And disturbed Glenn?

For the first time a prickle of anxiety began to make itself felt for Glenn. He could be hurt like anyone else. And he could make mistakes too. If he'd been taken by surprise . . .

He'd heard something. The hastily stubbed out cigarette had told her that.

She went down the side path and paused. There was a light in the garage. A thin beam that was bobbing about like a firefly.

She crept to the window and cautiously raised her head. He wasn't hurt. He was holding the torch on something in his hand. Even in that light the diamonds glittered like liquid fire. He had Natalie's necklace.

10

THE torch went off without any warning. Glenn must have seen her head silhouetted against the window. She marched to the door and flung it open wide, turning on the harsh overhead light of the garage.

He stood looking at her without surprise. The necklace was no longer in his hands.

"Where is it?" she said abruptly. "And don't, please, feed me any more lies. If you imagine my father had anything to do with taking it again you couldn't be more wrong. Natalie and I last saw that necklace only a few hours ago in the office safe. We watched my father lock it up and he hasn't been alone for more than a few seconds ever since. And don't suggest he had an accomplice. That necklace was left here to incriminate him, nothing else. I suppose it was fairly easy to find."

"What are you doing up at this time of the night?"

She stared at him, exasperated beyond measure. "I was watching, as you were. Did you see that man plant the necklace?"

"What man?"

"Oh, stop treating me as though I'm an idiot. I saw a man leave here."

"Did you recognise him?"

"No, I didn't. It's dark. Maybe you hadn't noticed."

He stood looking at her, his face quite expressionless. "Don't you believe me?" she asked flatly, and when he didn't answer she said, "There's an agency man watching the house. I think he must have seen him too. He'd got out of his car."

"Wait here." He moved past her and she let him go. Would he have taken the necklace with him or left it where he must have found it?

The car door was open. She searched briefly; and couldn't find it. It looked as if he'd taken it with him. Well, that was all right. Anything was all right so long as the police didn't find it here.

She went out of the garage and down the path again. Glenn was bending down at the window of the car she'd seen the man enter. As she watched he straightened up and began to walk towards her, the light from a street lamp turning his hair to silver.

She was immediately back to that first night of her father's return, seeing again that dark figure with its suggestion of menace. The walk was unmistakable, the silent easy movements of an animal on the hunt.

"You were watching that first night," she flung at him as soon as he was near enough to hear. "I saw you. With a dog. Did you hire it for the part?"

"A friendly stray," he said casually. "Fortunately dogs take to me. They come in very useful at times. Let's go inside." He took her arm.

"Don't you touch me." She tried to pull herself away from him but his grip was firm.

286

"Don't be silly. I want to talk to you."

"Silly!" She snorted but allowed herself to be led back into the house. There was no danger of falling asleep now. She was vitally alert. She dropped the macintosh on the floor and shed the old shoes.

Glenn sat her down before the fire and switched it on, pouring out a glass of the brandy. "You must be frozen. Haven't you been to bed at all?"

"No."

"You didn't trust me?"

"You haven't exactly given me any reason to trust you," she said bitterly. "What did Mr. Gant's man say?"

"He saw the man and followed him to the end of the avenue. He had a car parked there. He didn't follow; his brief was to watch the house. He felt he might have acted unwisely as it was."

"Did he get the number of the car?"

"Oh, yes."

She relaxed. "That's all right then. I bet it turns out to belong to Miles."

"Yes."

"Yes? You mean you finally believe my father is innocent?"

"It looks that way."

"Well . . . ! Thank you for nothing."

"Melody . . ." He turned away from her and poured himself a drink. "I think you know what my job is, don't you?"

"I've got a very good idea," she said guardedly.

"Oh, more than that surely." He turned to look at her. There was a faint smile on his face. "You're a very transparent person. Travis told you. I thought he might. But I also thought he'd beg you to keep quiet about it and you would refrain from telling your father. You are a very loyal person. I'm sorry I had to deceive you. I had no choice—not while there was a chance your father took the jewels."

"I worked that out for myself," Melody said coldly.

"And what else did you work out?" His voice was very soft, a mere whisper of sound.

She clasped both hands around the

288

glass and stared into the artificial flickerings of the fire. "Lots of things," she muttered.

"Such as?"

"Such as the fact that you used me quite cold bloodedly. You meant me to fall in love with you."

"But I told you that. Remember? I was honest with you there. I was going to pull out of the job. And then you were kidnapped and I knew I couldn't let that happen again. I knew I was in love with you."

Melody squeezed the glass so hard it slid out from her hands. She stared blindly at the liquid running out over the carpet and then slowly she raised her head and looked at Glenn.

He hadn't moved. She couldn't have heard right. She said vaguely, "I must get a cloth," and rose to her feet.

"Never mind that." He caught her hand and drew her towards him and she knew her ears hadn't deceived her. His eyes were steady, his hands gentle. She gave a faint sigh and offered no resistance as his lips came down on hers and then she thought of Kate and it was like a douche of cold water enveloping her from head to toe.

She pulled away. "I almost forgot. I have a message for you. From Kate. She asked me to give you her love and said she'd be down at the cottage for the next three weeks—just in case. I don't know what she meant by that rider but I'm sure you understand."

She didn't wait for his reaction. She rushed upstairs and bolted into her bedroom.

He didn't follow her. After a long time she got into bed. Her mind was churning. What a stupid thing to do. Why run away? What was she afraid of? If he loved her he'd finish with Kate. Wouldn't he? She tossed and turned. She didn't know him. She couldn't make any sort of guess at what he would do. He hadn't followed her. He didn't care to explain.

She fell asleep as the sky started to pale and the faint twittering of birds started up under the eaves and it felt like the last day on earth when Michael shook her awake the next morning.

She didn't hear what he said at first. Her head was aching and she felt as if she'd been drowning in her own tears.

"Do you hear me?" The frantic note in Michael's voice cleared away the clogging mists and she blinked hard.

His eyes were burning bright.

"They're arresting father," he cried. "They've got a search warrant."

"No!" She flung herself out of bed and flew down the stairs, pushing rudely past a uniformed policeman.

Her father was putting on his overcoat. He was pale but composed. "Don't worry, Melody," he said steadily. "This time it will be all right."

She skidded to a halt, staring wildly around the room. Two men were emptying the bookcase, another was turning out the drawers in the sideboard. Bolton was watching dispassionately.

"You can't do this," she cried. "You can't!"

"We're doing it." His gaze went over her rudely.

"We can prove my father had nothing to do with it this time. We watched him lock up the jewels and he's not left this house for a second."

"What jewels are you talking about, Miss Ford?"

"Oh, don't try to be clever with me," she cried hotly. "It's perfectly obvious what's happened but this time we were ready for it. We baited the trap. We have witnesses to prove my father's innocence."

"So prove it."

She stared at him and then moved abruptly to the phone. There was no reply from Natalie's flat. She listened to it ringing, on and on. Where was she? She couldn't be out. Not now.

"Come along," Bolton said to her father.

"Wait. Wait." She put the phone down. "Where's Glenn?"

Aunt Prudence answered her. She was standing stiffly in the corner of the room, holding herself upright with an effort. "He wasn't here when I came down this morning."

"He can tell you. He had the necklace last night. A man left it here to incriminate father."

Bolton's mouth turned down in a sneer of sheer disbelief. "You'll say anything, won't you?"

"But it's true. It's all true."

He turned away from her, his hand on her father's arm.

Melody ran forward and flung herself in her father's arms. "Don't worry. We'll have you out in no time. They won't lock you up again. Not ever. And they'll be apologising. They'll be sorry they did this to you."

He held her close, his hands stroking her hair, and then Bolton pulled him away.

She felt a desperate ache inside her. Her father had thought she was talking wildly too. She'd seen it in his eyes. The utter hopelessness. There was no fight in him, not this time. He saw it all happening again. His worst fears were realised.

She went back to the phone. There was still no answer from Natalie's flat. "I don't understand," she said in a low voice. She glanced at the clock. It was almost ten. "Oh, why did you let me sleep on?"

"We weren't expecting the police," Aunt Prudence said dully. She was looking at the mess they had left behind them. Sounds from above indicated that they were doing the same thing there.

"What were you talking about?" Michael said in a strained voice. "Baiting a trap and saying Glenn had the necklace?"

"He did, he did. Oh, where is he? And where's Natalie?" Melody felt like crying. This wasn't turning out at all the way they had planned.

"I'll make some tea." Her aunt turned in a stricken fashion towards the kitchen.

"No, wait." Melody couldn't bear to see her looking like that. "It's going to be all right, I promise. They'll have to let him go. Listen . . ." The words tumbling over one another, she told what Natalie had done. "So you see," she finished. "They won't be able to hold him for long."

Her aunt didn't look convinced. Michael demanded belligerently, "Why didn't you tell us before?"

"It had to be this way. Everything had to seem normal."

"Natalie asked you to keep quiet, didn't she?"

Melody's eyes fell away from her aunt's shrewd gaze.

"I don't blame her," she said with a sigh as Melody didn't answer. "I can see why she would want your father to remain in ignorance. Doubt is a deadly thing in your mind." She started to replace the books on the shelves. "You'd better get dressed. I think they've finished upstairs."

The sound of the men coming down was unmistakable. It was like a herd of elephants on the move. They trooped out of the house without a glance in their direction.

Melody moved to the window. They'd started on the garage. Her heart was in her mouth until they'd finished but they didn't find anything.

She went upstairs and put on her slacks and a thick sweater. It would take her the morning to clear up her room. She thought bleakly of the storm this would have raised if they'd done it in anyone else's house. They had no redress. Her father was a criminal in everyone's eyes.

But not for long. Not now.

She tried Natalie's number again. There was still no reply but almost as soon as she had replaced the receiver it rang and she recognised Natalie's voice.

She hardly allowed her to get a couple of words out. "They've arrested father," she cried. "They've taken him away."

"Oh, that's fine," Natalie said as if she'd said it had stopped raining. "I want you both to come out to the cottage. There's something I have to show you."

"Natalie! Don't you understand.

Father's been arrested. The police were here just now and they wouldn't listen to a word I said."

"No, don't bring anyone else," Natalie said conversationally. "Just you and your father."

Melody felt a thin trickle of coldness down her spine. "There's something wrong, isn't there?" she said slowly.

"Yes, dear."

"Someone standing over you?"

"That's right. You'll stay for the weekend. I must go now, Melody. Take care."

Melody replaced the receiver blindly. "They've got Natalie," she said blankly. "They want father and I at the cottage."

She turned and looked at her aunt and Michael. "What shall we do?"

Her aunt's face puckered. She had lost her air of brisk efficiency with the arrival of the police. "The police?" she said tentatively.

"They won't believe me. You know that."

"What about this detective agency?" Michael suggested. "Won't they help?"

"Yes. Ring them. Mr. Gant is the man in charge. Explain." She went into the hall and pulled her anorak off the peg.

"Where are you going?" her aunt faltered.

"To Natalie."

"But—but you'll be walking right into a trap."

"If I don't go they'll suspect Natalie warned me in some way. They might kill her, especially if someone else turns up instead." She zipped up her anorak. "I might be able to distract their attention, do something anyway—until help arrives."

"You're a fool," Michael said bluntly. "What do you imagine you could do? A mere girl!"

"A mere girl can do a lot of things," she snapped. "Don't you underestimate me."

"I'll come with you."

"Oh no, you won't." Her voice softened as she saw him stiffen. "No,

298

Michael. They'd think it odd. Besides Gant will need someone to show him the way. You can remember it, can't you, and the layout of the house?"

"Of course I can," he said scornfully.

"Then that's your job."

Aunt Prudence had the telephone directory out. "I can't find his name in it," she cried. "It's not under Gant. There are no Gants at all."

"Let me see." Melody grabbed the directory but her aunt was right. She closed her eyes. Natalie had said Gant. She was sure she had. But the agency could be listed under another name.

She dialled the shop number. If Miles answered she didn't know what she'd do but it was a woman who spoke and she recognised the breathless, slightly foolish tones.

"This is Melody Ford," she said. "Can you give me Mr. Gant's number? It's urgent."

"Yes, of course." There was a subtle difference in the voice, a calm, steady certainty that had nothing foolish in it.

She reeled the number off and said, "Trouble? Can I help?"

"Keep your eye on Miles. He might try to make a run for it." She rang off and handed the phone to her aunt with the scribbled number. "It's up to you now. Convince him."

She was backing the car out of the garage when Michael came dashing out of the house. "Here," he said. "I've filled it with ammonia." He thrust a water pistol through the car window. "Well, it's better than nothing," he said defensively as she blinked at him.

"Yes." She swallowed hard and slipped the pistol in her pocket. "Thanks, Michael. It will probably come in useful."

"You'll be careful, won't you?"

"I will." She smiled at him brightly. "Just you bring up the cavalry with all speed."

"Don't you worry." His lower lip was thrust out pugnaciously. She swallowed again. The lump in her throat was threatening to explode. She could see him standing there long after she had turned the corner. He had grown up this last week. But then so had she.

She drove like the furies to Kensham, turning in at the driveway without hesitation and stopping the car at the front.

The imposing door stood ajar. She pushed it open and walked through into the hall, calling out Natalie's name.

"In here, Melody." Natalie's voice was unsteady. It came from the sitting room.

She took a deep breath. She had to be believed. It wasn't to be taken as a trick. "Something terrible has happened," she began. "They've arrested father. He—" She stopped in her tracks. She had entered the room and no one was there but Natalie. She was sitting stiffly on the couch.

Then the door closed quietly behind her.

She spun round.

It was Hartley.

And there was a gun in his hand.

"What did you say?" he said menacingly. He was dressed in an ordinary business suit. The gun looked most incongruous and out of place. She stuck her hands in the pockets of her anorak and felt for the water pistol. "I said my father has been arrested," she said in faltering tones. "W-what are you doing with that gun?"

"He's a desperate man," Natalie said in a tone that dripped ice. "He's lost all his money and he has to get out of the country fast. I suspect that more than the police are after him. He saw the jewels as his stake for a future in foreign fields."

"Are you all right?" Melody backed away from Hartley as a jerk from his gun indicated that she should sit on the couch beside Natalie.

"*I* am. But Tom has a bullet in his arm. He made him drive us all the way down here and then when I refused to phone you he started on Tom. He would have killed him. I'm sorry, Melody. I had to do it."

"Where's Tom now?"

"He's locked him in one of the rooms with the rest of the staff. He's quite mad. He has to be to act like this."

"He's alone then? There's no one with him?"

"He is quite alone."

"Shut up both of you," Hartley shouted. "I've got to think."

"Poor man," Natalie said sardonically. "He needs peace and quiet. Well, he'll get plenty of that. I take it you informed the police, Melody?"

"No." Melody gave a warning shake of the head at Natalie but it was too late. Hartley pounced on her. "You knew! You knew I was here!"

"No!"

"Don't lie to me. You warned her somehow. You bitch." He lashed out at Natalie with the gun and struck her across the side of the face. She was knocked sideways. Blood streamed from a gash in her cheek and she stared at him dazedly as he raised his hand again.

"Leave her alone," Melody cried.

"You'll get your father here. At once. Or else!"

"But he *has* been arrested. I wasn't lying."

303

He hit Natalie again and she moaned and then lay very still.

"There's one thing I've learned," Hartley said heavily. "People like you resist talking when they're hurt themselves but they can't bear to watch someone else suffer. Now where's your father. Tell me or I'll really start on her."

Melody bowed her head in her hands. She needed time to think but Hartley wasn't giving it to her. "He's outside," she said unevenly. "I dropped him at the bottom of the driveway."

"Is he alone?"

"Yes."

"You're sure?" He grabbed Natalie by the hair and pulled her to a sitting position. She moaned again but didn't open her eyes.

"I'm sure," Melody cried. "I knew it was no use going to the police. They wouldn't help. They won't do anything for us because they think my father is a criminal."

"All right." That made sense to him. He brought the gun down hard on

Natalie's head and she collapsed without a sound.

He smiled at Melody. "I don't like excess luggage. Remember that."

"You might have killed her," Melody breathed, leaning over frantically to feel for Natalie's pulse.

He struck her hand aside and pulled her to her feet. "Not her. She's a tough one. I just want her quiet for a long time. Now take me to your father."

The long drive had shrunk. He marched her down it, tightly gripping her arm, his gun at the ready. "What was your idea?" he demanded.

"Idea?" Melody said vaguely. She had no ideas. Her mind was quite blank.

"You must have had some plan in mind."

"Oh! Plan!" She realised what he was getting at. "We weren't absolutely sure something was wrong. My father was going to ring for help if I didn't come out for him."

"Who was he going to ring?"

"Well—er—the local police. They

wouldn't know who he was. He could have got them out here with some excuse. And if he sees me coming along with you like this he'll know something is quite definitely wrong."

"Are you suggesting I let you go on ahead?" he said with heavy sarcasm. "He won't rush off when he sees you. Not him. He'll be too concerned."

"He will. He'll see there is nothing he can do. *He* doesn't have a gun."

"Where did you leave him?"

"Oh—at the gate."

It was around the next corner. Hartley stopped. "Ford!" he shouted. "I've got your daughter here. If you're skulking in the bushes you'd better come out, otherwise she's going to get hurt." He fired the gun at the sky. "Do you hear me? The next one goes in her."

"He's probably already gone for the police," Melody said, her heart in her mouth. She couldn't see how she was going to string this out any longer. Where was Gant? Why was he taking so long?

"You'd better start praying he hasn't,"

306

Hartley said. He raised the gun and then lowered it again as the sound of a car hit his ears. It was travelling at speed.

He jerked Melody to the edge of the driveway, the gun thrust into her neck. "If this is the police, you're for it."

It wasn't the police. It was Glenn. He stopped the car beyond the gate and got out. "If it isn't Sir Galahad himself," Hartley sneered. "What's he doing here?"

"I don't know." Melody's wits completely failed her. "Maybe my father called him instead."

"And he came by jet?" Hartley raised his voice. "Come on forward. Don't be shy." An unnecessary invitation as Glenn was already walking steadily towards them but he stopped when Hartley snapped, "That's enough. What are you doing here?"

"I brought you this. Interested?" Glenn put his hand in his pocket and Hartley hastily moved the gun away from Melody and pointed it at Glenn instead. "Watch it. Pull that hand out slowly."

Glenn did so. Maddeningly, almost

painfully slowly. And the necklace dangled in his hand like a living snake.

Hartley's breath caught in his throat and he took a step forward, his hand falling away from Melody's arm, allowing her to get the water pistol out of her pocket. She pointed it at his face and closing her eyes pulled the trigger.

There was no scream of anguish; no reaction whatsoever. She opened her eyes. The pistol might have been empty but Hartley sensing movement behind him, whirled, and she knew *his* gun was loaded.

She hurled herself to the ground at the same moment as he pulled the trigger. When she raised her head again Glenn was holding Hartley's gun hand and they were fighting desperately for control.

Her face met the ground again as the gun went off once more. This was dangerous. She had a frantic urge to crawl to the nearest ditch and cower in it until it was all over. She could be hit. She might have been hit already. She'd read somewhere that there was a period of numbness before the nerves reacted to pain. She was certainly numb. All over.

She picked up the water pistol and looked up the barrel. There seemed to be an obstruction there. She shook it and then blew down it and then pointed to the ground and pulled the trigger. This time a thin stream of ammonia shot out. She felt the pungent odour hit the back of her nostrils, catching her breath.

She hopped around them, wishing they'd stay still for just a moment. Hartley was fighting like one possessed. Some half dozen times she had the pistol pointing in his direction and then he had rolled over and gained momentary mastery. She lost patience in the end and took a hand herself, grabbing his hair and squeezing the trigger.

He screamed, clawing at his eyes, the gun forgotten, and Glenn picked it up and rolled back off him, coughing as he got to his feet. "I've not blinded him, have I?" Melody said anxiously, looking down at the writhing figure.

"It won't last." Glenn wiped his eyes

with the back of his hand. "You're a dangerous woman. Where's Natalie?"

"Up at the house. He knocked her out. And shot Tom in the arm."

He lifted his head. "It sounds as if the reinforcements have caught up with us. Go along. I'll join you later."

It was much later before she saw him again. Robert Gant had brought some half dozen men with him and was quite chagrined to find everything was all over. Both Tom and Hartley were taken to hospital. Natalie insisted she was all right. She wanted to get to the police station and would have got there if she'd been dying on her feet.

In the early evening Melody's father was allowed to leave and the police were directing their attention to Miles, whose car number did match the one taken by Gant's operator.

The film was disappointing. Glenn arrived as it was being shown for the second time in Natalie's flat. It showed Miles opening the safe, the time clock recording it was one twenty seven a.m. but the necklace was the only item he took out.

"It beats me," Gant said. "The equipment can't be at fault and yet there's not another thing on that film."

"I'd like to see that safe," Glenn said slowly.

Melody's father looked at him and then he was on his feet. "We'll go now."

It was a curiously tense moment as Glenn bent down in front of the safe. He leaned forward. They had seen Miles lean forward like that in the film. But it wasn't the necklace he brought out. It was the big leather case belonging to Natalie's friend. He leaned forward again and Natalie uttered a soft cry. "My jewels!"

Glenn straightened up. "They must have been there all the time," he said. "A double safe! I've seen one before. No thief would look beyond the obvious. They're skilfully concealed, operated by pressure applied at particular points. I don't suppose Mrs. Mathieson even knew what her husband was doing when he supposedly discovered the jewels were missing."

"I had no idea that was there," Melody's father said uncertainly, as if expecting no one would believe him.

Glenn smiled at him. "No. I think we'll find he had it installed when you were away. He'll crack now." He took the jewels from Natalie. "I'll take care of these. Just for the time being."

"You mean until I return the money." Natalie smiled but let them go with some reluctance. "Well, you've got what you wanted now, haven't you?"

"Not quite all." His eyes were on Melody.

Natalie's gaze narrowed. "I can't say you surprise me. Well, Peter . . . You can't provide the slightest excuse for not marrying me now. I've risked my life for you and I insist you do the right thing. We'll all go back to my place to celebrate."

"But—" he began and then smiled, glancing at Melody. "You see how it is."

"I see exactly how it is," she said laughing at him. "You'll be very happy and you know it."

312

"Maybe," he said dubiously, but his eyes were warm and happy again.

Natalie took him firmly by the arm. "There is no maybe about it. Now come on, everybody."

"We'll join you later," Glenn said catching hold of Melody's hand and stopping her from following the others.

Natalie glanced over her shoulder. "I thought maybe you would," she said smilingly. "But if you decide to carry her off again do let us know this time."

"I'll send you a telegram." He closed the door behind her and cupped Melody's face in his hands. "Kate is my cousin— nothing more. Do I have to do as Natalie suggests or will you come willingly this time?"

"You told Aunt Prudence you had no family," she said accusingly.

"And neither I have—not in the way she meant. Well, Melody? Which way is it to be? There's no escape. You're mine now."

"In that case . . ." She sighed luxuriously, "I surrender," and she went into his arms. There were no more shadows, no doubts, no fears or suspicions. The hunter had caught his quarry and would roam no more.

THE END

Other titles in the
Linford Romance Library:

THE MOUTH
OF
TRUTH

by Isobel Chace

Deborah's father disapproved of her plans to go to Rome with her boy-friend, Michael, but she simply defied him. However she had hardly set foot in Rome before she was whisked away by Domenico Manzu, who kept her in his palace. But why?

PINK
SNOW

Edna Dawes

In Austria in search of a folk-tale for her next book, Kathryn Davies is soon caught up in a chain of events which lead to an attempt on her life. Soon it is apparent that the villagers of Mosskirch are conspiring to involve her in murder, and she does not know who she can trust.